Next stop . . . an open grave!

Skip leaped to his feet. The bus veered. It threw Skip across the aisle. He fell on top of another kid.

A hand dripping foul green slime caught his arm. "Hey," a voice rasped in his ear. "Watch where you're falling."

Skip turned and got a faceful of dead breath from a creature that had once been human. But no more. It looked as if it were melting, its puke-green flesh trickling in disgusting waxen blobs from its face, its hands, even its ears.

Reeling back, Skip felt something clasp his shoulder. "Wh-What are you?"

"A ghoul," said the creature.

Skip tore free and turned to run. He stopped. He gasped. He gagged.

He was surrounded by them. Creatures from beyond the grave.

Other Skylark Books you won't want to miss!

GRAVEYARD SCHOOL

The Tragic School Bus

Tom B. Stone

A SKYLARK BOOK

New York   Toronto   London   Sydney   Auckland

RL 3.6, 008–012

THE TRAGIC SCHOOL BUS

A Skylark Book / September 1996

ISBN 0-553-48490-7

Published simultaneously in the United States and Canada

PRINTED IN THE UNITED STATES OF AMERICA

OPM   0 9 8 7 6 5 4 3 2 1

GRAVEYARD SCHOOL

The Tragic
School Bus

CHAPTER
1

"This house is haunted," said Skip Wolfson. "Definitely haunted."

His brother, Mark, froze. "H-How can you tell?"

"I thought you had good eyes. You don't see that ghost?" Skip pointed toward the dark end of the hall.

Mark whipped around. "Where?"

"Stop it, Skip! Your brother is only teasing, Mark. Now get upstairs and finish unpacking," Mrs. Wolfson said.

"There's no ghost?" asked Mark.

"Not anymore," muttered Skip.

"Skip!" Mrs. Wolfson warned.

Skip stopped. He knew that tone in his mother's voice. It meant he was bound to get in trouble if he didn't stop. He might as well quit while he was ahead.

Mark looked as if he didn't know whom to believe, his older brother or his mother. His face was filled with suspicion and fear.

Not a bad expression for the little monster, thought Skip.

"Finish your breakfast," Mrs. Wolfson went on. "You don't want to miss the bus."

Yes, I do, thought Skip.

"We better not be late for school!" A new fear had replaced Mark's fear of ghosts. "Dr. Morthouse *hates* kids who're late."

"Dr. Morthouse is your principal. The principal doesn't hate anybody," their mother answered.

"Yes, she does," said Mark. "She hates puppies and kittens and babies and kids and apple pie, and she has a silver fang in her mouth."

"Mark! Where do you hear things like that?" Mrs. Wolfson gave Skip a sharp look.

"Not from me," said Skip. "Everybody knows about Dr. Morthouse's fang." Inwardly, he revised his wish about missing the bus. If he missed the bus, he wanted to miss school, too.

A meeting with Dr. Morthouse at any time was unfortunate. A meeting with her because of being late was potentially fatal. Skip didn't know for sure if it was a deadly experience or merely a near-death one, since he had never been late to Grove Hill Elementary School. And he didn't want to find out now.

After all, the students called it Graveyard School, and not just because an ancient, abandoned graveyard stood on the hill behind the school. The general weirdness of

2

people like Dr. Morthouse contributed to the name, not to mention the strange and truly terrifying things that happened at the school.

Of course, the adults never seemed to notice. So even if it was true that a kid who had once been late three days in a row had been caught on the fourth day by Dr. Morthouse and had never been seen again—whom could you ask?

The adults would just deny it.

Skip gulped down the last of his orange juice and jumped up from the table. "I'll go to the corner and wait for the bus," he announced.

"I didn't mean you had to rush through your breakfast," said Mrs. Wolfson. "You've still got plenty of time."

"I've gotta go, too," Mark said, looking like he was about to freak. "Okay, Mom?"

"Not until you've finished everything on your plate," she answered firmly.

"And it's your turn to feed Lupe and give her fresh water," Skip added. Lupe was their dog. She was sitting next to Mark, watching with a hopeful expression as he ate. Hearing her name, she thumped her tail.

Mark began to eat as fast as he could.

"Oink, oink," said Skip.

"Tell the bus to wait for me," Mark mumbled through a mouthful of oatmeal.

Grabbing his backpack, Skip made for the door. "In your dreams," he said, and slammed it behind him.

3

A low mist hung over the fields that surrounded their new house. Or rather, their old house—the old farmhouse that his parents had just bought.

"A growing boy needs room to roam—and play," their father had said.

"Isn't it beautiful!" their mother had exclaimed.

"Cool," Mark, the nerd-in-training, had said.

"We're in the middle of nowhere, in case you haven't noticed," Skip had said. "Can we move back to civilization soon? Like, immediately?"

But of course his parents didn't listen to him. They never did. So now Skip lived in the middle of nowhere, miles from anything, in a creaky old farmhouse that should have been haunted, even if he didn't really believe it was.

He took a deep breath and choked. This was fresh air? It smelled like manure.

He staggered down the rutted driveway to the narrow, bumpy road.

No bus. Just fields and corn and pastures and cows that mooed and did other obnoxious things. He wrinkled his nose and headed down the road toward the corner where the bus was supposed to stop.

The farmhouse his parents had bought was on Post Road—once a main road that connected the town of Grove Hill to another main road. But it was a dead end now. It ended somewhere beyond their farmhouse, just over a hill. Post Road was a road that went nowhere.

4

Thinking of this as he walked toward the bus stop, Skip made a face. He lived in the middle of nowhere on a road that went nowhere. Pathetic.

Skip turned to see if his brother had made it out of the house yet. No sign of the little monster.

He turned back and kept walking. Post Road might have been paved once. And only once. The road buckled and sagged and lacked pavement altogether in numerous places. It was easier to walk on the grass next to it than pick his way along it.

A cow mooed. A bird called.

Gag me, thought Skip. The cow leaned against the fence that ran along the road and mooed again. Mushy grass trailed from her mouth, shifting from side to side as she chewed.

"Get a life," said Skip.

The cow turned her head. She looked past Skip, up the road behind him. She stopped chewing. She began to back away from the fence.

"Boo, moo," said Skip, and laughed. The cow ignored him. She just kept backing up. Her legs moved stiffly. She looked like a cow in a video game with bad graphics.

Skip laughed harder. Then something made him stop laughing. Something made him turn around.

He wasn't alone anymore. His eyes narrowed. A cloud of dust was coming over the top of the hill along Post Road.

A tractor? A farm truck? But there was only one other house on the road, a farmhouse across from the Wolfsons' and farther up the hill.

Where had it come from?

The dust swirled higher. The cow had backed herself into the midst of the other cows. They'd stopped mooing. Stopped moving. The herd bunched together warily.

The birds stopped singing. The breeze disappeared.

Blinding morning sun glanced off something bright in the midst of the cloud of dust, and Skip blinked.

When he focused again, he saw a school bus emerging from the cloud.

As the bus passed the foot of his driveway, he realized that his little brother was probably going to miss it.

Be late for school.

Spend some nasty quality time with Dr. Morthouse.

The thought cheered Skip up somewhat. He shifted his pack and raised his arm to flag down the bus.

The bus seemed to shift gears. It lurched. The huge front windows glittered, almost like eyes. Tornadoes of dust spun from the wheels. The bus picked up speed.

"Hey!" shouted Skip indignantly. He stepped a little way into the road and waved both arms above his head.

Closer. Closer. Faster.

"Hey, speed kills!" Skip called. He made a rude gesture at the bus.

The bus swerved toward him.

"You jerk!" shouted Skip. "Watch it!"

The bus seemed to roar toward him. Only it wasn't roaring. It wasn't making any sound at all. In the whole motionless, muffled world, the bus was the quietest thing of all. Completely silent.

Ghastly silent.

Ghostly silent.

Skip panicked. He turned and began to run.

Dust puffed up around his feet. It blew into his face and filled his mouth. He couldn't breathe.

When he looked over his shoulder at the bus looming above him, just before he went down, he thought he saw a green claw morph through the windshield and reach for him.

Then he fell, and the bus rolled over his body.

CHAPTER
2

"Skip? Skip! Why are you in the middle of the road? Get up or you'll miss the bus."

Mark's voice seemed to come from far, far away.

Skip rolled over. His arm made a crunching sound, as if a hundred tiny bones were being ground to dust.

My arm, he thought. *I broke my arm.*

"And why are you lying on your backpack? You just broke your potato chips into a million pieces," Mark added.

With a groan Skip opened his eyes, expecting to see the greasy underside of a school bus above him.

His brother's face swam into view. Skip sat up. He pushed his brother away.

"I'm not dead yet," he said. "So keep back, dog-breath."

"You're going to *get* dead if you stay in the middle of the road," Mark retorted.

Skip looked down the road. No bus. No dust. No tire marks.

He looked up the road.

Empty. No sign that a bus had ever been there.

He got to his feet. "Did you see the bus?" he asked.

"What bus? We didn't miss it, did we?" Mark's voice went up in panic.

As if in answer to his question, a bus roared into view along Valley Road. It roared and wheezed and groaned. It sounded like a fat, yellow insect gorged on students.

"Oh, nooo!" Mark wailed. He jumped over Skip and began to run as fast as he could toward the bus stop.

Skip scrambled to his feet and took off after his brother.

He saw the bus draw up next to the bus stop. He saw the doors open. Mark, the little traitor, jumped on without a backward glance.

"Hold on!" Skip shouted, "I'm coming!"

Skip was sure the bus wouldn't leave him. It was probably against school bus law or something.

The doors of the bus began to close.

With a last, desperate sprint, Skip reached the bus. He managed to get his fingers between the doors. For a moment he thought the doors would close anyway, dragging him to school by his fingertips.

But at last the doors opened slowly. A voice as rusty as the bus's engine snarled, "Get in."

Skip scrambled onto the bus. "Thanks a lot," he said sarcastically.

The doors closed.

"Siddown," the bus driver ordered. He threw the bus into gear with a clash of metal, flinging Skip down the aisle. Skip lurched, staggered, and fell across Kirstin Bjorg's lap.

Someone made a kissing sound. Skip pushed away and slid into the seat next to Kirstin, his face red.

She brushed off the legs of her jeans. "You're covered with dirt," she said in a bored voice.

Catching his breath, Skip said, "What're you doing on the bus? You always ride your bike to school."

Kirstin Bjorg was class president, a killer soccer player, and generally unmoved by anything, like human emotion. Graveyard School had that effect on a lot of kids.

She looked even more bored. She yawned.

"I mean, I didn't know you lived this far out of town. It's too far to ride your bike," Skip went on.

Kirstin shrugged. Then she said, "I decided to ride the bus for a change." She turned to look out the window.

"Siddown in back," snarled the bus driver without turning his head.

"How does he do that?" a voice said from behind him. Skip turned to see Ken Dahl sitting in the seat behind him. Like Kirstin, Ken had blond hair and blue eyes. Unlike Kirstin, he didn't have a clue.

"It's like he's got eyes in the back of his head," Ken went on.

Skip looked toward the bus driver, a tiny, wizened man with a baseball cap pulled low on his forehead.

"They install them in the maintenance shop," said Skip. "Extra eyes."

Ken gaped. "Really?"

Skip snickered. So did Kirstin.

"Oh," said Ken. He made a face. "That was a joke." He sat back, pouting.

Surveying the bus, Skip realized that he didn't really know anyone on it, except maybe by sight. He decided he didn't really want to know anyone on it, either.

He cleared his throat. As casually as he could he said, "By the way, did you happen to see another bus this morning?"

Kirstin turned from the window to stare at him.

"Another bus? Out here?" asked Ken, leaning forward again. "Like a city bus?"

"Like a school bus."

"No." Ken shook his head. "No other bus comes out here. Hardly anything comes out here. We're outside the city limits."

"I know this is the outer limits," Skip said. "Believe me."

It was a feeble joke, but it drew a snort from Kirstin. "Did *you* see another school bus?" she asked.

"Oh, yeah. Up close and personal. Like it ran over me." Skip paused and frowned. "Or at least, it almost did."

"No way!" exclaimed Ken. Then he frowned. "Is that a joke?"

"It's no joke, Ken. It really happened."

Ken eyed Skip suspiciously.

Kirstin raised one eyebrow. "That's why you're covered with dirt then," she said. She was quick. Skip had to hand it to her.

"Yes."

"No tread marks, though," said Ken, still looking suspicious.

"Ken, if I had tread marks on me, I'd be dead," Skip said. He suddenly saw himself lying in the road. Saw himself sitting up. And in the picture in his memory, realized that the road itself, dusty as it was, hadn't had a single tire mark on it—just his footprints, and Mark's.

Kirstin said, "It couldn't have been a real school bus. This is the only school bus that comes this way."

"I know what I saw," said Skip. But suddenly he wasn't so sure. He felt a chill creep up his back, as he remembered the silent bus. And the green claw that had pushed against the windshield.

No. He'd imagined the claw. He'd panicked and imagined it.

But he couldn't have imagined a whole bus.

He looked up to find Kirstin watching him. "I know what I saw," he repeated.

"Huh," said Ken, and leaned back again.

"Interesting," murmured Kirstin, and turned back to the window.

Forcing a smile, Skip checked the bus out again. Everyone looked pretty average. Just a bunch of kids on a trip to Graveyard School. Just another ordinary school day.

So why was he suddenly so afraid?

The sense of doom haunted Skip for the rest of the day. When the heavy hand fell on his shoulder in the cafeteria lunch line, he leaped into the air with a scream that made everyone in the lunchroom turn to stare. He flung his tray into the air, too.

Fortunately, he hadn't gotten any food yet.

"Hey," said Tyson Walker, snagging the tray. "Awesome vertical."

"Ha, ha," Skip answered sourly.

"But poor sense of humor," Tyson added.

Skip jerked the tray out of Tyson's hand and pushed down the line.

"Ah, a big selection today," Tyson commented. "Glop, slop, and—what is it? My favorite: garbage."

14

A cafeteria worker glared at Tyson. Tyson smiled back. "I'll have the garbage special," he announced. He pointed to what might have been macaroni casserole.

When they reached their table, Jaws Bennett was already chowing down. Jaws was famous because he could eat anything—even, he bragged, roadkill.

So far, the lunchroom hadn't served roadkill. But watching Jaws chomp his way through what the lunchroom passed off as human food, Skip decided that Jaws wasn't making an idle boast.

Sitting at the table with Jaws, Algie Green, a skinny kid with glasses who wore his hair pulled into a small ponytail at the nape of his neck, and Park Addams, baseball fanatic, were also eating lunch. They were eating it much more cautiously than Jaws.

"How's life in the bus lane?" asked Park. He lifted something unidentifiable on his fork and passed it down to Jaws. Jaws ate it. Park thought it was funny that Skip had to get up at dawn now to ride the bus.

"I'm not sure," said Skip.

Ken said, "Skip almost missed the bus. The bus driver doesn't like that. It's a bad way to begin riding the bus. The bus driver never forgets."

"Thanks for the tip, Ken," Skip said.

With a flick of his wrist, Tyson sent his roll in Jaws's direction. He gave Skip a sympathetic look. "Tough ride, huh?"

Tyson knew how Skip felt about the Wolfson family's

big move to the middle of nowhere. It was only thanks to Tyson that Skip could still make soccer practice after school, catching a ride with Tyson when Skip's parents couldn't pick him up.

Having to ride the school bus was ruining everything. Not to mention the fact that it had almost been fatal.

As casually as he could, Skip said, "Well, the only tough part was when the bus almost hit me."

That got everyone's attention. They all stared at Skip.

"Cool," Tyson said at last. "What happened?"

"I was walking to the bus stop and the bus came down the road and almost hit me," Skip said.

Ken was frowning, concentrating hard on what Skip had said. Then he said, "No, it didn't. You had to run down the road to get to the bus stop so the bus wouldn't leave you."

"Not your bus. The other bus," said Skip.

Frowning harder, Ken said, "There *isn't* any other bus. I told you that."

"I thought you lived on a dead-end road," Tyson said. "Does the bus stop right in front of your house and then turn around?"

"No. The bus stop is down the hill from my house, where Post Road meets Valley Road," Skip explained. "That's why I was so surprised to see the bus behind me. I had just come out of my driveway, and I was walking down Post Road to the bus stop."

Algie stopped eating. He put his fork down slowly. "Isn't Post Road out near Seven Mile Hollow Road?"

Skip shrugged. "I dunno."

Ken said, "Yeah, it is. Only the bus doesn't stop there. And there's only one bus."

"Today, this morning, there were two buses," Skip snapped. "I know what I saw."

Algie looked from Ken to Skip, then back again. "What did the bus look like?"

For a moment Skip had a vision of the green claw, the windows like big bug eyes, the sinister, silent rush of the bus over the rutted road toward him. "It was . . . ," he said. He stopped. Then he shrugged again. "It was just a school bus. Big. Yellow. Ugly."

"But it didn't *really* hit you, did it?" Park asked. "I mean, if it had, you'd be dead, right?"

"Yeah, I guess," Skip admitted.

Tyson said, "Good thing. You would've missed soccer season for sure."

Park lost interest. "Soccer," he said scornfully. "Forget soccer. What he wants to play is baseball. Right, Algie?"

But Algie, who had a wicked curveball from hours of practice throwing newspapers on his afternoon paper route, was staring at Skip with a troubled expression.

"Seven Mile Hollow Road," he muttered. Then he said, "Be careful, Skip. Be very, very careful."

17

"Yeah. Or you'll get busted. Bus-ted—get it?" Park laughed again.

Everyone else laughed, too.

Even Skip managed a smile.

Everyone except Algie. "Be careful," he said again softly. Then he got up, picked up his tray, and left the table.

CHAPTER

3

"So this is Skip," a voice croaked.

Skip stopped in the doorway to the kitchen. A small woman of no particular age, wearing a jeans jacket, a flannel shirt, a faded pair of overalls, and enormous, battered work boots, was sitting at the kitchen table across from Mrs. Wolfson. Both of them were holding mugs. Skip recognized the smell of peppermint tea, undercut by another newly familiar smell.

Cow manure.

He caught a glimpse of fur under the table and realized that their dog, Lupe, had also smelled the cow manure and was pressed against the unfamiliar woman's boots. Lupe probably thought the visitor smelled great.

"Yes," said Mrs. Wolfson. "This is Skip. Skip, this is Mrs. Strega, our neighbor. She's the one who sold us this house."

"Gee, thanks," Skip muttered.

His mother gave him a sharp look. Fortunately, Mark started talking before Skip could get in trouble.

"Those are Mrs. Strega's cows," Mark said excitedly. He was sitting at the end of the table, staring at Mrs. Strega in delight. "The ones in the field across the road."

Skip didn't bother to say that he'd already figured out that Mrs. Strega had a close association with cows.

"Can I pet one sometime?" Mark asked.

"Sure," Mrs. Strega told him. Her skin was brown and deeply lined. Her dark brown eyes had a sharp, shiny look, as if they didn't miss anything. She turned her attention to Skip and said, "Hello, Skip."

"Hello," Skip said.

"Mrs. Strega's lived here forever and ever," Mark said.

Mrs. Strega chuckled. "I'm not that old. The farm's only a couple of hundred years old, you know. But it has been in my family the whole time."

"How was soccer, Skip?" asked Mrs. Wolfson. "Would you like a snack?"

"Fine. No thanks," Skip answered. He'd had a hard day. He'd found himself looking over his shoulder as he walked through the dusk from the foot of the driveway where Tyson's mom had dropped him off. He'd half expected to see a school bus come roaring out of nowhere to make skid marks up his back.

Now that he'd reached the house safely, he just wanted some peace and quiet.

"I'm kind of tired," he added, so that his mother wouldn't think he was being rude and get on his case after Mrs. Strega left.

The farmer put her mug on the table. "Gettin' late," she announced. "I've got chores to do."

"Are you going to feed the cows?" asked Mark, bouncing in his seat.

Mrs. Strega smiled. A net of fine wrinkles spread out around her eyes, and Skip realized that she was older than she had first appeared. "And the chickens, too."

"Can I help sometime?" asked Mark.

"Of course," said Mrs. Strega. "Long as you don't chase any of 'em."

Mark looked hurt. *He's such a literal-minded little dweeb,* thought Skip.

Their mother got up. "Let me get you one of our business cards and a price list," she said. The Wolfsons ran a pet supply store in the town of Grove Hill. They'd recently expanded into farm supplies. She left the room.

"Matter of fact, you can come over anytime. I'd come before dark, though," Mrs. Strega said to Mark.

"Why?" asked Skip, in spite of himself. He thought he saw a malicious gleam in the farmer's brown eyes. But he couldn't be sure.

"So you won't run into the ghosts," she said calmly.

"There's no such thing as a ghost," said Skip, annoyed at being teased like a little kid.

"But this morning you said you saw a ghost," said Mark. "You said this house was haunted."

Mrs. Strega looked at Skip thoughtfully. "Did you, now?" she asked.

"I was just *kidding*," Skip said.

"Post Road was a busy road before they closed it off," Mrs. Strega said, as if she hadn't heard Skip. "Enough happened along this road to account for more than one ghost."

Mark's eyes widened. "Wow," he breathed.

Mrs. Strega nodded. She lowered her voice and leaned forward. "When I was growing up, I used to hear things, see things . . ."

"Like what?" asked Mark.

"Well . . ."

"Here you are," said Mrs. Wolfson cheerfully, coming back into the kitchen.

The farmer straightened up. She pushed her chair back and stood. "Thank you," she said. She nodded toward Mark and Skip. "You come over and visit now," she told them. "Don't be strangers."

The two women walked to the front door.

Mark stared after them. "Ghosts," he said softly.

"She was just yanking your chain, Mark, okay?" said Skip.

He turned and stomped upstairs to his room. Great.

Their closest neighbor in the country was a loony old farmer who believed in ghosts.

"Cow manure," muttered Skip. He slammed the door of his room behind him.

"It's a great idea, right?" said Mark. He let a handful of silverware slide onto the kitchen table.

"Sure," said Skip. He wasn't really listening. He was thinking about ghosts. He was thinking about the silent school bus that had almost made tread marks up his back that morning—the school bus that no one else had seen.

"You really think Mrs. Strega will let me help her feed her cows?"

"Before you can even say 'Old MacDonald had a farm.'" Skip handed Mark the plates and began to arrange the silverware.

"She has chickens, too, remember?"

"How could I forget? And I bet you better not mess with her chickens. Farmers shoot dogs who mess with their chickens. Hear that, Lupe?" Skip looked down at Lupe, sitting between the kitchen table and the refrigerator, one of her favorite food-stalking points.

Mrs. Wolfson came in and ruffled Mark's hair. "Nobody's shooting anybody, Skip. I think it's a great idea for Mark to help Mrs. Strega."

Mark beamed. Then he stuck his tongue out at his brother.

"Gosh, that hurt," said Skip.

"Go wash your hands," their mother said. "Your father will be home any minute now."

Mark cannonballed out of the room with Lupe on his heels. Skip turned to follow.

And a terrible scream split the air.

CHAPTER
4

Skip grabbed the edge of the kitchen table so hard that his knuckles turned white.

The screaming stopped.

"Wh-What was that?" Skip said.

Mark turned to look over his shoulder at his brother. He cocked his head. Mrs. Wolfson began to pour water into the glasses on the table. "What was what?" she asked without looking up.

"That—The—That scream," stammered Skip.

"What scream?" asked his mother. This time she did look up. She stared at Skip, puzzled.

"That scream! That horrible scream! You must have heard it!"

"*I* didn't hear anybody scream. Did you, Lupe?" Mark said from the doorway.

Lupe wagged her tail and cocked her head.

"What is this? Some kind of a joke? Someone screamed!" Skip insisted.

"Maybe it was the wind, Skip," Mrs. Wolfson said in her reasonable-mother voice. "These old houses make all kinds of noises when the wind is blowing."

Skip could still hear the echo of the scream in his ears, a sound of pure terror, as if someone had seen something unimaginable. Something horrible.

Then another sound registered on Skip's reeling senses, a hammering sound.

"Someone's at the door," he said.

"It's Dad!" shouted Mark, wheeling toward the back door.

"The front door," said Skip.

"I didn't hear the doorbell," Mrs. Wolfson said.

"Someone's *knocking,*" said Skip. "At the front door."

Mark cocked his head again.

Their mother said, "Well, can you answer it? Maybe Mrs. Strega forgot something."

Skip remembered that Mrs. Strega had left by the back door. Why would she use the front door now? For that matter, why wouldn't she use the doorbell?

The hammering continued, frantic now.

"I don't hear anything," Mark insisted.

"You don't hear that, dogfood-breath?"

"Ha," said Mark. "You can't scare me. You're just making it up, like the ghost. C'mon, Lupe." Mark turned and ran out of the kitchen.

The knocking echoed through the house. Skip put his hands to his ears and headed for the front door.

He grabbed the doorknob. *"Owww!"*

Grabbing it had been like touching dry ice—so cold that it burned his hand.

He slid the sleeve of his sweatshirt down over his hand and grabbed the doorknob again.

The knocking stopped abruptly. Eerie silence replaced it.

Skip flung the door wide.

No one was there. Beneath the yellow porch light, all was silent and still. Still as a grave.

The hair on Skip's neck rose. He licked his lips. "Who's there?" he croaked.

No one answered. Nothing moved. Not even a breath of wind stirred the trees.

"Who's there?" he said more loudly. "Who is it?" He was about to step out onto the porch, but something stopped him. It was so dark out there beyond the light. So dark.

"Who is it?" said his mother's voice behind him.

"No one," said Skip. "No one's there. I guess it was some kind of a joke."

Mrs. Wolfson stepped past him onto the porch. Skip flinched, half expecting something to swoop out of the darkness and grab her.

But nothing did.

His mother looked around for a moment. Then she turned and came back into the house. She closed the door behind her.

She looked at Skip. "Listen," she said. "I know you didn't want to move here, Skip. But I think you'd like it if you'd give it a chance. So let's call a truce, okay? No more ghost sightings, no more trying to scare your brother. No more jokes."

"It wasn't a joke," said Skip. "I *did* hear someone scream. And someone really *was* knocking on the front door."

"Skip," said his mother in her reasonable-mother-about-to-lose-patience voice. "We live too far from our neighbors for anyone to run up onto the front porch and knock on the door and then just run away again."

"Mrs. Strega could have just pretended to leave," Skip said desperately. "Then she could have screamed, and knocked at the door, and then run away."

His mother was shaking her head. "Mrs. Strega didn't do anything of the sort, and you know it, Skip."

Skip looked down at his hand and saw the red burn on the palm. He looked at his mother's hand, still resting on the doorknob.

"But . . ."

His mother let go of the knob. "Go wash up for dinner," she said, and left him standing alone in the hall.

Cautiously he reached out to touch the doorknob.

It felt like an ordinary doorknob, neither cold nor hot.

He looked down at his hand again. The red mark was gone.

"Ooodle-oooooohhh . . ."

Skip bolted upright in his bed, then fell back again. No one was screaming. It was a rooster.

"Cockadoodle-dooooooh . . ."

"Shut up," he muttered. Naturally, the bird ignored him. It had a job to do. Dawn would come at any moment.

Dawn. Skip groaned and pulled the pillows over his head.

"Skip! Rise and shine!" A fist thumped his door.

He lifted the pillow and called back, "I don't have to get up yet. School doesn't start for hours!"

"The bus will be here before then. And it won't wait for you," his mother called back.

He yawned again and got out of bed. He decided to try to stay asleep while he got ready for school. He wondered if he'd be able to sleep on the bus.

He was still yawning when he went out the back door and headed for the bus stop with Mark trailing beside him. Just as it had the day before, mist was curling off the fields. A scarecrow grinned at them crazily from across the road, its arms laden with raucously cawing crows.

A thin sheet of dew clung to the little three-sided metal and plastic shed that served as the school bus stop. Skip closed his eyes and leaned back against one side.

He heard the grinding of gears as the bus approached the last hill on Valley Road before the Post Road bus stop.

"It's here!" said Mark.

"Thanks, bone-breath," said Skip, opening his eyes.

The bus clipped the top of the hill, two wheels rising off the road and coming down heavily. It gave a mighty shudder and swerved toward them.

It was a rude awakening. "Look out!" Skip shouted, and grabbed his brother's arm. He yanked Mark out of the bus stop and into the ditch and fell in after him.

The bus slid to a halt. The doors opened.

Skip struggled to get out of the ditch. He lost his footing in the mud and fell backward.

"Owww!" Mark howled.

Strangely distorted faces peered down at them through the grimy windows. The doors of the bus began to close.

"No. Wait!" Skip panted. He got to his feet and almost fell again. But he managed to turn his fall into a forward lurch up the side of the ditch.

The doors closed. The bus slid away.

"Wait!" Skip shouted. "Hey! You can't do that!"

The bus could. It did. It rattled over the hill and out of sight.

"What'dja do that for?" Mark whined.

"Because it almost hit us," Skip said. He reached down and grabbed his brother's arm and yanked him out of the ditch. "You stink," he said. "You're covered in mud."

"So are you," said Mark.

It was true. Their dive into the ditch had been a dive into a slimy, sticky mudbath. Even if the bus had waited, they couldn't have gone to school.

Mark shivered. "I'm cold."

They were standing there coated in muck, surrounded by fog. The sun had come out, but the morning wasn't really warm yet.

"C'mon," said Skip. "Let's get back up to the house and get some dry clothes on."

Their mother was not thrilled to see them. Mark's explanation—"Skip saw the bus and pushed me into the ditch"—didn't help matters.

"This is not funny," Mrs. Wolfson said.

"I wasn't trying to be funny," Skip said.

She pursed her lips. "Get changed and I'll drive you to school." Skip could tell she didn't believe him, could tell that she thought he had done it on purpose.

"We could miss school," said Mark hopefully.

Skip was glad to see that his brother was at least a little human. But he wasn't glad about the look he got from their mother.

"I'm sure Skip wouldn't want to do that. Would you,

31

Skip?" she asked. Before Skip could answer, she said, "No. Better late than never, I always say. Isn't that right, Skip?"

Better dead than late, thought Skip. But he knew better than to answer. He kept quiet.

At least it was a real bus this time, he thought.

The steps leading to the school were ominously empty.

"You're not *so* late," said their mother, pulling her pickup to a halt. "Out you go."

"Aren't you going to write us a note?" asked Mark.

"Nah. You're not late enough for that. Just explain what happened. I'm sure your teacher will understand."

It wasn't the teacher Skip was worried about, it was the principal.

He slid out of the truck and followed Mark as he scampered up the stairs. Skip looked uneasily around. They were so exposed. Was Dr. Morthouse lurking, waiting for them behind the big old entrance doors? Watching them from her office?

They were sitting ducks, easy targets out there on the stairs. But inside . . .

Skip stopped at the top of the stairs and stared hard at the school doors. He wished he had X-ray vision. Or even a keen sense of smell. Dr. Morthouse probably had a distinctively dangerous scent, like a mountain lion or a grizzly bear.

He sniffed the air experimentally. But it was no use.

"Come *on*, Skip," Mark said. "What are you doing?"

Skip sniffed again, then gave his brother a hopeful look. "You have a good sense of smell, dog-brain—do you smell anything?"

Mark sniffed. "No. Like what?"

"Like Eau de Principal," said Skip. Seeing his brother's puzzled look, he explained, "Like anything that smells like Dr. Morthouse . . . oh, never mind."

He walked resolutely up to the doors. He pushed them open.

He ducked.

Nothing happened.

The halls were empty and quiet. Murmurs came from behind the nearby classroom doors. The door of the principal's office was open, but no one was in sight.

So far, so good.

They walked softly down the hall, keeping close to the walls. They got to the end of the hall where Mark turned left to go to class and Skip turned right.

Mark paused.

He sniffed.

"What is it?" Skip said.

But Mark didn't answer. He just hunched his shoulders and melted into the shadows of the hall that led to his class.

The hairs on Skip's neck stood up. He sniffed.

Eau de Principal. It had to be.

He turned. And came eyeball to lapel with a dark gray suit and a row of ivory-colored buttons.

Skip blasted off from his sneakers so hard and fast that he might have rebounded off the ceiling, except for one thing.

The hand that came down like an iron claw on his shoulder.

CHAPTER
5

"Well, well, well. If it isn't Mr. Wolfson." Dr. Mort-house's voice poured over Skip like boiling oil. Skip looked up, winced, and looked down. The glint of silver in her smile was blinding.

"You can call me Skip," he said to the second jacket button of her gray suit, then looked up at her face again.

Dr. Morthouse's eyes narrowed. He hadn't realized it was possible for them to get any smaller or meaner. "Are you trying to be funny?"

"No! No," said Skip hastily. Why did everyone these days think he was trying to be funny?

Life wasn't funny. Life was dangerous.

Like now. Standing in the hall of Graveyard School with his shoulder in the principal's death grip, his face only inches from the flash of her fang.

"Good," Dr. Morthouse purred. "And you aren't try-ing to sneak into class late without a pass, are you . . . Skip?"

"No! I mean, we, uh, I didn't know I was late. But my mom said if there was a problem . . ."

"Your mom?" asked Dr. Morthouse in a silky voice. The iron grip loosened fractionally on his shoulder. "I see. And your statement is that your mother *knows* you were trying to sneak into class late?"

"Yes! No. I wasn't trying to sneak in. I mean, she said if I was late, to explain . . ."

"Should we give your mother a call, do you think?" Dr. Morthouse's fingers tightened and loosened and tightened again, the way a cat's claws flick in and out as it toys with its prey. Each time her fingers tightened, Skip felt a quiver of fear run through his spine.

He straightened his shoulders. He forced himself to look up.

He quickly looked down again, locking his eyes on Dr. Morthouse's suit buttons. He tried to concentrate on those. *Very strange buttons,* he thought. *They look almost like little tombstones.*

"No," said Dr. Morthouse at last. She turned him and began to propel him forward. "No, I'm going to let you go this time, Skip. I think you made an honest mistake. And I'm sure you're sorry. I'm sure you'll never, ever be late again."

"Yes. An honest mistake. Very sorry. Never, ever late again," Skip heard himself babbling. *You dweeb,* he thought. But he couldn't help it. He was still babbling

36

mindlessly when Dr. Morthouse opened his classroom door and steered him through it.

Faces turned toward them. Ms. Watson looked up from her roll book and drew her brows together sharply.

A murmur rose from the class.

And died when Dr. Morthouse smiled.

"Hello, boys and girls," said Dr. Morthouse.

Perfect Polly Hannah suddenly giggled. She was that kind of girl.

The principal didn't seem to notice or care. She smiled at Ms. Watson. She released Skip. "Have a nice day, Skip," she said in a voice that made fingernails on a blackboard seem like the sound of music. Skip stumbled to his seat and fell into it.

Ms. Watson gave Skip a reproachful look and went on with the roll call.

"Skip got in trouble, Skip got in trouble," Polly Hannah singsonged under her breath.

Leaning forward from the desk behind Skip, Tyson whispered, "Is this your unlucky day or what?"

"Skip Wolfson," Ms. Watson read from the roll book.

"Yes," said Skip. He leaned forward and pressed his forehead against his hands.

Life doesn't get any worse than this, he thought dully.

He was wrong.

*　　*　　*

The truck was waiting for him after soccer practice. Skip saw it the moment it pulled into the parking lot. Who could miss a truck painted in forty shades of green, covered with pictures of the earth, and emblazoned with screaming blue letters that said THE ANIMALS' HOUSE—PET SUPPLIES ON THE GO! on the side?

The truck honked. Skip kicked the ball toward the open goal—a sure shot, a perfect score.

He missed the ball completely and fell on his back.

"Thanks," said Tyson, sliding the ball sideways and out of reach of Skip's foot—and the goal.

The coach blew the whistle. Practice was over.

The horn honked again. "Yo, Skip, your ride's here," said Tyson.

Skip got up. "Thanks, Tyson," he said sarcastically.

Tyson pretended not to notice. "No problem. Nice wheels."

At least I don't have to ride the bus, thought Skip, gathering up his gear. He glanced toward the truck.

His parents were not normal. Skip knew that. But this was beyond not normal. His parents' love for their new delivery truck went into the deeply weird. Beyond the Twilight Zone.

"Dad," he said, opening the door. "Next time, don't honk."

His father concentrated on shifting gears as Skip fastened his seat belt. The truck made a grinding noise, then leaped forward.

Skip slid forward, then slammed back against the seat. *Good thing I'm wearing my seat belt,* he thought grimly. *I only sort of broke my neck.*

They careened out of the parking lot. After several more grindings, his father succeeded in getting the truck into the proper gear.

"Why?" he asked Skip.

Skip released his white-knuckled grip on the seat's edge. "Why what?"

"Why don't you want me to honk?"

"Because the colors on this truck are so loud, I can hear you without the horn," said Skip.

He wasn't trying to be funny. He meant it.

But his father laughed. "They *are* a little bright," he said. "But it's good for business. People remember us."

"I know," muttered Skip. "I know."

"How was school?"

"Fine."

"I heard you missed the bus."

"Mark has a big mouth," said Skip.

His father wrestled with the steering wheel, and they tilted around a corner. "You have to be responsible about catching the bus, son," his father lectured. "Living as far out as we do means we have to leave early ourselves to open the shop for early deliveries. Expanding our business means we—"

"—all have to work together," Skip finished for him. How many times had he heard this lecture? "I know, I know." He changed the subject. "I could have gotten a ride home with Tyson. You didn't have to pick me up."

"My pleasure," said his father.

Skip changed the subject again. "You know, if I had a motorcycle, I could ride that to school. Maybe even give Mark a ride."

"You're not old enough to have a motorcycle," said his father.

"I'm almost old enough," said Skip. "If I got one now, I could start practicing. Learn how to drive it. Country roads are good for that."

"We'll talk about it when you're old enough," Mr. Wolfson answered.

They turned down a dirt driveway and pulled up in front of a small barn. Two guys in overalls came out and met Mr. Wolfson as he jumped out and opened the back of the truck.

Skip folded his arms, closed his eyes, and leaned back against the seat. He stayed that way as his father started the truck and maneuvered it back up the driveway. "A little extra help is always welcome," his father said, to no one in particular.

"I'll tell Mark," said Skip.

"Watch it," his father warned.

Skip yawned. But he didn't make any more smart remarks. He maintained a safe, dignified silence. It had

40

not been his lucky day. No reason to assume that his luck would change now.

"One more delivery," his father said. "Then home for dinner."

Skip yawned again. His father gave him a sharp look, then turned his attention back to the road.

Resolving not speak, Skip let his eyelids droop. A bad day. An unlucky day. But it was almost over now. All he had to do was keep quiet and—

Skip's eyes flew open. He bolted upright in the seat. *"Dad!"* he screamed. *"Look out!"*

CHAPTER
6

His father slammed on the brakes. Without thinking, Skip grabbed for the steering wheel and yanked it.

His father yanked it away.

"Look out! Look out!" Skip shouted frantically.

"Let go!" his father shouted back, wrestling with the wheel. The truck veered across the road and tipped sideways.

The school bus leaped toward them.

"Look out!" Skip screamed one last time. He threw up his hands and braced himself for the crash.

A shudder passed through his body.

The school bus vanished.

Mr. Wolfson wrestled the truck back into its lane. He steered it to one side of the road. With elaborate caution, he pulled up the parking brake and turned off the ignition before turning to Skip.

"*What* is going on?" Mr. Wolfson demanded angrily.

"The b-bus," Skip stammered. "Didn't you see it? The school bus?"

"What school bus?" his father answered. "The only thing I saw was you jumping up out of nowhere and grabbing the steering wheel! You almost made us have a wreck!"

"But Dad, it was a school bus. It was going to hit us head on!" Skip's heart was still pounding in terror. But his father didn't look terrified. He just looked angry.

"I didn't see a school bus because there wasn't a school bus. The bus finished its route hours ago," said Mr. Wolfson.

"But it almost *hit* us. You had to have seen it!" Skip was almost shouting again.

His father took a deep breath, as if he was maintaining control of himself with an effort. "Are you saying that we just almost hit a school bus?"

"Yes!"

Mr. Wolfson shook his head. "We didn't. There's no one on the road but us, Skip. No cars. No trucks. And no school buses." He paused, then held up his hand as Skip opened his mouth to protest. "This isn't your idea of a joke, is it, Skip? Because if it is . . ."

Skip balled up his fists in frustration. "No!" he cried. "It was a bus. A school bus. It was coming right toward us!"

"Then where did it go?" asked Skip's father in the

44

voice of a father trying to be reasonable. "If it was coming right toward us, why didn't it hit us? Where did it go?"

Skip looked wildly around. It was true. They were the only ones on the road. The only ones anywhere in sight. He couldn't even see any cows.

"It was right there!" Skip pointed. "I saw it!"

Mr. Wolfson reached over and put a hand on his son's forehead. Skip pulled away. "I'm not sick," he said.

"No fever," Mr. Wolfson said to himself. He stared at Skip. Then his expression brightened. "Of course," he said. "You were almost asleep. You'd been yawning. You *dreamed* you saw a bus."

"It wasn't a dream," said Skip. "It wasn't."

But his father wasn't listening. He released the truck and started it. "You really scared me," he said, steering the truck back onto the road. "If that ever happens again, son, whatever you do, don't grab the steering wheel. That is very, very dangerous."

"But—"

"You could have gotten us killed! What if I hadn't been able to keep control of the truck? We could have hit a tree! Turned over in the ditch."

"But—"

Mr. Wolfson glanced at Skip.

Skip swallowed hard. He sank back against the seat. "Okay," he said. "I'm sorry."

His father patted Skip's knee, satisfied. "That's okay. Now, try to stay awake, will you?"

"No problem," said Skip, forcing himself to smile.

He was telling the truth. It was easy to stay awake. His heart was pounding. His head was spinning. He scanned the road, watched the rearview mirror, turned to look over his shoulder. He even scoped the fields.

The bus had come out of nowhere. And disappeared into nowhere.

But he'd seen it. And he was going to be prepared when he saw it again.

They pulled off the road onto a gravel driveway under a faded sign. Skip could make out the word TOURS on the sign, but not much else in the last light of the afternoon sun.

A door opened and a voice shouted, "Hey!" A short person jumped off the front porch of the house. A man came around the side of a garage, wiping his hand on an oily rag.

"Ken," said Skip.

"Hey!" said Ken again, running up to the truck.

"You know each other?" said the man, stuffing the oily rag into his pocket as he came up behind Ken.

"We're in school together," said Ken. "Skip just started riding the bus."

The two fathers shook hands. Skip got out of the truck reluctantly to help unload the order.

Mr. Dahl waved them away. "Show your friend

46

around," he said to Ken, and turned back to talk to Mr. Wolfson.

Ken studied Skip for a moment. Then he said, "C'mon."

Skip followed silently.

"You don't look so good," Ken said.

"No kidding, Sherlock," muttered Skip.

"What's wrong?"

Skip shrugged. He didn't want to talk about it. At least, not to Ken. Suppose he told Ken what had happened and Ken thought he was crazy?

"You lived here long?" Skip asked, to change the subject.

Now Ken shrugged. "Ever since I can remember," he said. "My father inherited it from some weird great uncle right after I was born."

"You like it?" Skip asked.

Frowning, Ken said, "I never thought about it. Sure."

They walked around the side of the barn, and Skip stopped in his tracks. The hair on his neck stood up. He raised a shaking hand and pointed. "W-What's that?" he asked hoarsely.

Ken gave Skip a sly glance. "Don't you know? It's a school bus."

"A school bus," Skip repeated.

"It's not really a school bus anymore," Ken said. "I mean, it's a piece of junk now. It used to belong to my dad's uncle. I used to play in it when I was a kid."

47

Skip walked closer, unable to believe his eyes. "The Curse of the School Bus," he muttered.

"What?" asked Ken.

"Nothing." The school bus was ancient. The tires were flat and rotten-looking. Weeds grew window-high along it in some places. Rust flaked and chipped away from the fading yellow exterior. The windows wore a layer of grime almost as thick as a coat of paint.

It couldn't be the bus I saw today, thought Skip. *Or yesterday.*

Still, it gave him an uneasy feeling. "Are you sure it doesn't run?" he asked Ken.

"What do you think?" Ken laughed. "Get in and give it a try."

Just then Skip's father called his name.

"No thanks," said Skip, secretly relieved. "Gotta go."

Skip and Ken walked back around to the delivery truck.

"That school bus you have out back," Skip said to Mr. Dahl. "It doesn't work, does it?" He ignored the sharp look his father gave him, and the funny expression on Ken's face.

Mr. Dahl snorted. "Nope. I should go on and junk it. But it's been there so long I don't notice it anymore." He looked at Skip's father. "Belonged to my great-uncle. He was one crazy guy. He bought the bus to start a tour

48

service. Out here in the middle of nowhere! Now *what* was he going to show people, I ask you?"

"Time to go," Mr. Wolfson said, looking at his watch. He smiled at Mr. Dahl, and they shook hands.

Skip nodded at Ken and climbed into the truck.

Get a grip, bus-brain, he told himself.

But he kept a sharp eye out for school buses all the way home.

CHAPTER
7

"What you've got here," said Tyson, "is a clear case of a ghost bus." He pulled up the hood of his gray sweatshirt and raised his arms. "Booooo," he moaned.

"Yeah, right," Skip said sarcastically.

"No way," put in Park. "A ghost bus? Give me a break."

"What else could it be?" Tyson argued. "It doesn't make any noise. It appears and disappears. It doesn't leave any tracks. And only Skip can see it."

"No way," Skip echoed Park.

"I read a folk tale once about this ghost dog that only howled before someone died," Tyson persisted. "And the only person who could hear it was the one who was gonna croak."

"Ghost dog? What're you guys talking about?" Stacey Carter came up the front steps of the school to join them, pushing aside the little kids who congregated on the lower steps as if they weren't even there. Maria

Medina was with her. Close behind them followed Polly Hannah.

Like the guys, Stacey and Maria were in jeans. Maria wore one of her huge collection of oversized rugby shirts and a jeans jacket. Stacey was in her dog-walker's uniform, her jeans tucked into her boots, a jacket with big pockets over her cropped sweater. Stacey worked as a dog-walker and pet-sitter to earn money.

Polly, as usual, was in a dress. This time it was flowered, with big pink buttons down the front. She was wearing yellow tights that matched her headband and flat shoes with flower buckles.

She stopped, folded her books in her arms, and pressed the books against her chest dramatically. "Who's talking about ghosts?" she demanded in her shrill voice.

Skip groaned. Great. That was all he needed—for the whole school to be talking about his being stalked by a ghostly school bus. He'd never hear the end of it.

Quickly he planted an elbow in Tyson's side.

Stacey saw him. Her eyes narrowed. They remained narrowed as Tyson said, "Uh, you know, a story I read for a report."

"A report on ghosts?" Polly said. "It sounds stupid."

Pushing her spiky bangs back, Maria said, "You should know, Polly." Maria didn't like Polly. Not many people did. Polly didn't like anyone at all.

"Very funny," said Polly. "So funny I forgot to laugh." She lifted her chin and marched up the stairs.

"Well?" demanded Stacey when Polly was out of hearing. "What's really going on?"

"Nothing," said Park quickly. Too quickly.

With one swift motion Stacey snatched the baseball cap from Park's head. She flipped it into the air and caught it.

"Hey! That's my lucky hat!" Park said.

"Not anymore," said Stacey. Park lunged for the cap. Stacey flipped it to Maria. Maria flung it like a Frisbee back to Stacey, keeping it just out of Park's reach.

Park stopped and turned to glare at Tyson and Skip. "Give me some help here," he complained.

Algie Green had locked his bike to the bike rack and had come trudging up the stairs. When Stacey tossed the hat to Maria, Maria dodged behind Algie, laughing.

"This is *not* funny," said Park.

From behind a bewildered Algie, Maria said, "Tell us what ghost you were really talking about or your hat *dies.*"

Algie frowned. He looked at Park. He looked up the stairs at Skip and Tyson and then over at Stacey. "Ghost?" he said.

Then he looked directly at Skip. "You mean the ghost bus you saw before school the other morning?"

Park stopped in his tracks, amazed. Maria walked out from behind Algie to stare at him.

Skip gaped at Algie. Ducking his head in embarrassment, Algie pushed his glasses up his nose with his forefinger.

"Did you say *ghost bus*?" Skip managed to ask at last. "How did you guess?"

"Kirstin told me," said Algie. Algie had been Kirstin's campaign manager after Kirstin had befriended him when he was the new kid in school.

"She told you I was run over by a *ghost* bus?" Skip asked. He heard his voice crack.

"No—just that you'd almost been run over by a bus. But there are no other buses out there," Algie said. He paused, then added, "And there are a lot of other weird things. It's only logical."

Algie should know, thought Skip. He'd had a paper route out that way one time, a paper route along Seven Mile Hollow Road. But he'd given it up for very good reasons.

Reasons that didn't bear thinking about.

"There is no such thing as a ghost," said Maria firmly. "Weirdos, wackos, and truly twisted people, yes." She glanced over her shoulder toward the door of the school, behind which their principal often lurked in the mornings, peering out at them. "But no ghosts."

"Just because you haven't seen a ghost doesn't mean

ghosts don't exist," Algie said in his mild way. "You can't see gravity, but we all stick to the earth."

"Yeah," said Tyson.

"If this bus is a ghost, what's it a ghost of?" Park asked. "I mean, why is it haunting Skip? I mean, it's tried to take him out twice now." Seeing the puzzled looks on everyone's faces, Skip told them what he had just told Tyson and Park about his second encounter of the big yellow kind with the bus the previous afternoon.

"Wow," said Stacey. "But you need proof."

"Right," Skip said. "Next time it runs me over, I'll write down its license number."

Stacey rolled her eyes. "Do you feel deathly cold when the bus comes near you? Cold is a sign that a ghost is nearby."

"That's true," said Tyson. "That's what it said in that ghost dog story."

"It *is* true," Algie agreed. He didn't cite his source. And no one dared ask him how he knew, not even Maria.

"I don't remember," said Skip. "I was too busy getting run over. Next time, though, I'll take a picture."

He was being sarcastic.

But Stacey's eyes lit up. "That's it!" she cried. She gave Skip an enthusiastic thump on the shoulder.

Park took advantage of the distraction to snatch his cap and resettle it on his head backward.

55

"What do you mean, that's it?" Skip asked crossly. "Like I'm going to carry a camera around, waiting for this bus."

But Algie and Tyson were nodding, too. Algie said, "Stacey's right. You can't take a picture of a ghost. So if you take a picture of the bus and nothing shows up, that proves it."

"And if you do get a picture, we'll have a clue," Maria said. "We can use the picture to figure out who's driving the bus."

Skip thought about this. It didn't sound like such a bad idea. "Okay," he said. "I'll do it."

The mist was doing its usual hovering maneuver above the grass. It was thicker than usual because Skip was out earlier than usual. The sun was barely up, and even the dust in the road was a little damp from the dew that still clung to the grass.

Skip yawned. He patted his pocket to make sure the camera was still there. It was.

He hoped his mom didn't mind his borrowing it without asking. It was a neat compact camera with an automatic flash and automatic focus. The automatic flash was important. Skip didn't plan on taking just one picture. He planned on taking a whole roll.

At least the birds were awake. *They make a lot of noise for how small they are,* he thought, wincing and yawning again. He looked around for the cows, but he didn't see them. They were probably still asleep.

So the cows got more sleep than he did. So what? He yawned again.

Even though he'd walked slowly, he'd reached the end of Post Road. He stepped up to the bus stop and looked both ways.

The sun glared at him from just above the trees. The road was empty.

Skip walked back up Post Road to the end of his driveway. He walked down the road again.

He heard the faint mooing of cows now and frowned. It was getting late.

Up the road. Turn.

He heard the slamming of a house door. Heard his brother's voice call "Bye!"

Great, thought Skip. If anyone could find a way to mess things up, Mark could. Plus he would be sure to want to know why Skip had a camera and to ask Skip a million stupid questions.

To which Skip would have only stupid answers. "Yes, it's a camera. No, you can't use it. No, it isn't for a school project. No, I can't tell you what I'm taking pictures of."

Skip walked back down the road toward the bus stop, mentally arguing with Mark.

Maybe that was why he didn't notice the sudden silence, the way the cows stopped mooing and the birds stopped singing.

Maybe that was why he didn't see the morning sunlight turn a chilly gray.

Icy cold enveloped him.

"Brrr," he said, putting his hands under his armpits to warm them.

Then he realized what he was doing. He spun, shoving one hand in his pocket to grab the camera.

He screamed.

And the school bus was upon him.

CHAPTER

8

"Skip? Skip?"

He was lying in the dust in the road with the camera pressed against his face. Through the lens, he could see his brother's face. Mark leaned closer, and his face blurred.

"Skip, why are you lying in the middle of the road taking pictures?"

Skip lowered the camera and sat up. His eye felt sore. Had he jammed the camera against it that hard? He couldn't quite remember what had happened. But he'd had a fleeting, blurred impression of a face peering down at him through a window of the bus.

A face with big teeth and tiny eyes and skin like soggy toilet paper.

Yuck, Skip thought. He shuddered.

"Is it for a school project?" Mark asked.

"Yes," said Skip. He bent to examine the camera.

Relief washed over him. He hadn't broken it. Then he saw that he'd used up all the film.

When had that happened?

"What about?" asked Mark. "What's your project about?"

Getting painfully to his feet, Skip looked up the road. He looked down the road. He looked at the cows, standing at the fence now, watching.

One of them mooed.

"See you at McDonald's," he snarled at the cow. He was in a very bad mood.

"Who are you talking to?" Mark looked around in bewilderment. "We're the only ones here."

"Never mind. Come on, or we'll miss the bus." Skip headed for the bus stop, shoving the camera into his pocket and attempting as he walked to make himself look a little less like roadkill. Mark trotted after him.

The bus was coming over the hill just as they reached the corner. Skip watched it suspiciously. But it pulled to a stop like a normal bus, and the doors wheezed open.

"What project?" Mark persisted. "What project are you taking pictures for?"

Skip looked back along Post Road one last time. It was empty.

"Transportation," he said, and pushed his brother up the steps onto the school bus.

*   *   *

"Just for, like, a little while," Skip begged. "You'll get it back before soccer is over. I promise."

Kirstin folded her arms. "Borrow Tyson's bike."

"I can't. He didn't ride his bike today. He had to leave school early."

"How do you know I brought my bike?" Kirstin asked.

"You weren't on the bus," said Skip. "And you've got soccer practice, so you don't need your bike."

"You've got soccer practice, too," Kirstin pointed out.

"I know. I'll be a little late. Tell Coach for me, okay?"

"Why?" Kirstin asked, but she began walking toward the bike racks.

Skip waited until she'd unlocked her bike. He grabbed the handlebars. "Something's developing," he said. "Thanks!"

He jumped on and pedaled away before she could stop him.

"Is that true?" Skip pointed at the sign. "Your photos in one hour or your money back?"

The guy behind the counter peered out at Skip from behind thick glasses. "Yeah."

"Then I want pictures in one hour," Skip said. He shoved the roll of film across the counter and looked at his watch.

"It could happen," the man said cynically.

"Thanks," said Skip. "I'll wait."

"Not here," the man said. "You make me nervous. Go away and come back."

"In an hour," Skip reminded him.

"Yeah, yeah, yeah," the man said.

Skip went outside. He walked down the street and around the corner and stopped. He thought about crossing the road to the next block to visit his parents' shop. Then he remembered that he was supposed to be at soccer practice.

At that moment his father came out of the pet supply shop, clutching a stack of papers. Skip made himself small against the wall of a building.

His father sorted through the pile of papers. Then he began to fold them and put them under the windshield wipers of cars.

Skip edged his way along the wall until he reached a door. He backed through it, keeping an eye on his father.

A bell tinkled. The door slowly shut with a wheeze that reminded him of the school bus.

Skip turned and froze. The hairs on his neck prickled in alarm.

He'd been in this shop before. Only it had been empty—except for a large, much too lifelike stuffed wolf in the window.

He spun around just as his father disappeared into a store across the street. A moment later he saw his father carefully taping up a sign in the window.

An advertisement for the new, expanded business, Skip realized.

Before he could make a break for it, his father emerged and began to leaflet more cars.

"Good afternoon," a voice said at his shoulder.

Skip made a sound between a scream and yip.

Someone behind him made a similar sound.

Turning, Skip saw a man no taller than himself. The man stepped quickly back, alarm in his eyes. He grabbed his scraggly mouse-colored hair with both hands and tugged it. "Don't *do* that," he complained. "You'll ruin my nerves."

"You scared me," Skip said.

"You scared *me*," the little man said, still holding on to his hair.

"Sorry," Skip said.

The man smiled suddenly. He released his hair. "That's okay." He held up one finger. "The customer is always right. What are you looking for? We don't get many young people in here. It's nice to see a gentleman of your age interested in old books."

"Books," Skip repeated, staring around him. He realized that he was in a bookstore, one that was filled from floor to ceiling, from wall to wall, with books.

Skip glanced back over his shoulder. Oh, no! His father was headed straight for the bookstore!

"I'm just looking," Skip said quickly.

"Well, let me know if I can be of any help. Any help at all—"

"Right! Sure. Definitely!" Skip plunged between two shelves of books and dodged out of sight just as the bell on the door tinkled again.

He heard the bookstore owner greet his father. He heard his father's voice murmur something in reply.

Skip looked around and saw an old chair in a corner next to the window. He flung himself into it, grabbed a book off the shelf, and held it up in front of his face.

His father and the bookstore owner continued to talk. Then, finally, the door opened, the bell tinkled, and the shop was quiet.

"Whew," whispered Skip. It wasn't that he was afraid his father would catch him. His father was a reasonable guy, for an adult. But Skip didn't think he'd be very reasonable about Skip's borrowing the camera and blowing off soccer practice to get a roll of film developed—especially a roll of film taken of a school bus that only Skip could see.

A bus that he'd almost wrecked his father's truck trying to avoid.

Although, given the extra high weirdness factor of his parents, Skip couldn't understand why his father didn't believe he'd seen an invisible bus.

He sighed. His eyes focused on the book. He was staring at the title: *A Short Tour of Grove Hill History.*

Hah, he thought sourly. *It would have to be short.* Nothing had ever happened in Grove Hill, at least nothing you could put in a history book.

He made a face.

Then he saw the photograph opposite the title page, and the hairs on his neck stood up again.

A man stood by a team of horses harnessed to a coach. He had one hand on one horse's halter. In the other hand he held an open pocket watch. He was scowling at the camera.

Across the street behind the man, two women in long skirts, large hats with veils and bows, and old-fashioned high-button shoes had been caught in midstride. A man in suspenders, also wearing a hat, stood in the shadow of a doorway, his coattails pushed back and his hands shoved into the pockets of his pants.

"Ancient history," muttered Skip, interested in spite of himself. He turned the pages of the book, wrinkling his nose at the old-book smell: dust and crumbling paper and glue turned to powder.

He found another picture of the man, now perched on the seat of the coach. At least he thought it was the same man. Only this time the man had a black patch over one eye. His lips were drawn back in a snarl at whoever was taking the photograph. Skip wondered if someone had told the man to smile.

The caption beneath this photograph read, "A Grove Hill mystery: Mad John, who drove his coach over a cliff—and was never seen again."

"Guess he missed the turn," Skip said. He'd begun to flip through the pages to look for more when the voice of the proprietor interrupted him. "Finding what you need?"

Skip looked up, barely preventing himself from jumping and screaming a second time. "Uh, yes." He held up the book. "How much is this book?"

The proprietor took the book and turned it over. "Good gracious!" he exclaimed. "How did this get back here?" He turned and scurried down the aisle.

Skip ran after him. "Wait," he said.

But the proprietor was unlocking a glass-fronted bookcase behind the counter at the back of the store. As Skip watched, he slid the book carefully into a niche on a shelf, then locked the case again. "A very valuable book," said the man. "The only one I know of in existence. Worth quite a bit."

"That old book?" Skip asked. "How much?"

"More than you can afford, I'm afraid," the proprietor said. "Now, may I help you with anything else?"

"Could I borrow the book? Just to make a copy of some of the pages?"

"Certainly not!" The little man looked indignant. "Cer-tain-ly *not!*"

"Is that a no?" Skip asked.

The little man lifted an eyebrow.

"But I need some stuff that's in there. For—For a report for school. On transportation."

"Then I suggest you use the library," said the man. He turned his back on Skip and busied himself checking the lock on the glass case.

"Thanks a lot," Skip said, with awful sarcasm.

"Don't mention it," the little man retorted, with equally awful politeness.

Skip scoped the street before he left. His father was gone, leaving behind a trail of leaflets tucked neatly beneath the wipers of cars. The bookstore had acquired a leaflet in its front window, too, Skip noticed.

Skip slammed the door behind him so hard that the bell sounded like a sleigh with eight tiny reindeer. He ran down the street to the photo shop.

"Where's the fire?" asked the man in the shop sourly.

"Where're my pictures?" Skip answered.

The man pushed an envelope across the counter. "No refunds no matter what the results," he announced as Skip snatched it up.

"I know, I know," Skip said, opening the envelope. The pictures spilled out.

"No refunds," repeated the man.

Skip didn't answer. He just stared at the photographs spread across the counter. He'd taken twelve pictures. The first one was of the sky and a bit of branch. The last was a blurred close-up of Mark's face leaning toward the camera.

The other ten photographs were blank.

Something wrong with the camera, thought Skip. *That has to be it.* He pedaled Kirstin's bike back toward school, hardly noticing where he was going.

He was halfway back to school before he realized he was being followed.

CHAPTER

9

He glanced back over his shoulder.

It was the bus.

Skip's foot slipped off the pedal, and the bike swerved into the road. He barely saved himself from being pitched headfirst over the handlebars. But he managed to get his foot back on the pedal.

He began pedaling much faster.

He looked back over his shoulder.

The school bus had picked up speed. But it hadn't come any closer.

Skip slowed down.

The bus slowed down.

Skip suddenly got angry. He turned the bike around and brought it to a stop.

The school bus stopped, too. Skip faced it, his heart pounding with fear and rage. "Hey," he shouted. "Hey, you! Go away!"

The bus didn't move.

"I'm not afraid of you," Skip lied. "See? Boo!" He got on the bike and pedaled a little way toward the bus.

He had expected the bus to move, to back up a little, keeping the same distance. But it didn't.

Its immobility unnerved him. He got off the bike and stared at the bus.

Was it real? Or was it a ghost? He wished he had another roll of film.

The afternoon shadows seemed to stir and lengthen as he stood there. A chilly breeze brushed the back of his neck.

"Go away!" he shouted again. "Leave me alone!"

Something about the way the bus just sat there told Skip that it wasn't going away. That if buses could be amused and contemptuous, this one was.

That did it. Skip jumped on the bike and, without thinking, pedaled straight at the bus. He screamed as loudly as he could, a war cry.

The bus didn't move.

Skip kept going. He was going to play this ghost game of chicken to the end. Even if it killed him.

Suddenly the bus leaped forward with terrifying swiftness and even more terrifying silence.

Skip screamed again, a different scream, as he collided head on with the ghost bus.

"Then what happened?" asked Park eagerly.

"I got up," said Skip.

Tyson nodded. "The bus went right through you. Ectoplasm can do that. Go right through your flesh."

"Gross," said Maria.

"Did you see anything? Feel anything?" Algie asked.

"Cold," Skip admitted. The cold had been bone-numbing. It had taken his breath away.

Stacey bent over the twelve photos fanned out on the lunchroom table and studied them, scowling in concentration. "Either you're the world's worst photographer, or your camera's broken—or you just took ten shots of a ghost," she said.

"He could be the world's worst photographer and still have taken pictures of a ghost," Maria pointed out.

Park laughed.

Skip glared at them. "It's not funny," he said.

"Sor-ry," said Park, not sounding sorry at all. He picked up one of the photographs.

"If you want to look at them in order," Skip said, "the first one is the one of the sky and the tree branch and the last one is the close-up of my brother's face. I'm not quite sure what order the other ten should be in."

After examining the photos for a long, silent moment, Park passed them to Tyson. Tyson lifted one eyebrow and softly said, "Whoa." He gave them to Algie, who glanced at them and winced before quickly handing them to Stacey.

"You took these when?" Maria asked.

"Yesterday morning. I had them developed yesterday afternoon."

"And then you got chased by the bus. Busy day," commented Park.

Before Skip could retort, Stacey said, "Well, that just proves one thing. You are definitely being haunted."

"I knew it. I was right," Tyson crowed. "Excellent!"

"Outstanding," agreed Park.

"I don't believe this," Skip said.

"I'm beginning to," said Maria. "I try not to believe in ghosts, but in this school . . ." Her voice trailed off as she looked over her shoulder.

Algie said slowly, "This is not good. Not good at all."

"Thanks for sharing," Skip snapped, exasperated.

"You don't know what kind of ghost it is—" Algie went on.

"Try a bus," Tyson put in.

Algie ignored him. "—whether it's good or bad. You don't know what it wants. You don't know how powerful it is."

"I haven't exactly had a chance to ask," Skip said. "Mostly, before I can say anything, it just runs over me."

"That's good, isn't it?" Stacey asked Algie. "I mean, Skip hasn't been hurt, at least. If it were a bad ghost, it would have hurt you, wouldn't it?"

Algie nodded thoughtfully. "True. Unless it isn't

strong enough yet. I mean, maybe your encounters with the bus, Skip, are just practice runs."

"Ha, ha," said Skip.

"Did you notice anything different about this encounter?" Tyson asked.

"The cold," Skip said instantly. "Right before the bus ran over me—"

"Or through you, actually. I think it's safe to say that's what occurred," said Algie.

"Whatever. It was cold. Really, really cold." Skip paused. There was something else. But what? He couldn't remember. It had all happened so fast.

"Maybe you should write down everything that's happened," suggested Algie. "Then you could remember better, especially if you wrote about it right after it happened."

"Maybe," said Skip. He looked around at his friends. "That's it? That's the best suggestion you can come up with?"

The bell rang. Lunch period was over.

Park stood and picked up his tray. "Yep. Just go with it, you know? I mean, as long as the bus isn't trying to turn you into a ghost, what's the problem?"

Skip sighed and stared out the window. It was a dark and gloomy night. If the sliver of moon had risen, it had been sucked up into the still, heavy darkness.

The knock at his door made him jump. Everything made him jump these days. When he wasn't being run over by ghost buses, he was jumping out of his skin expecting to be. "What!" he said.

"Night, dear," his mother said, poking her head around the door. "Don't stay up too late working on that report."

"No," said Skip. "Night."

"Night, son," his father called from the hall.

"Yeah," Skip muttered.

The door closed. Skip stared at the computer screen.

"Skip!" His brother knocked and opened the door at the same time. "What's that?"

"Homework," Skip said. "Mom!"

"I'm not doing anything," protested Mark.

"Yeah, but you're doing it in my room."

"Is it a secret project?" Mark asked.

Instinctively Skip covered the screen with his hand. "No. Go away."

Mark took another step into the room. Skip took a deep breath. "Mo—"

"I'm going, I'm going," Mark said. He slammed the door behind him.

Pipes rumbled. Voices came to Skip faintly through the old, thick plaster walls of the farmhouse. A toilet flushed. He heard his brother shout, "Night, Mom. Night, Dad. Night, Skip."

The house grew quiet.

Skip began to type. Now the only sound was the faint humming of his computer, the sticky click of the keys.

It got later. The house got colder.

Skip blew on his fingers for warmth and kept typing. He had just finished typing in everything that had happened when he'd tried to take photographs of the bus, when he heard it.

A faint, anguished wail.

Skip looked up. He couldn't tell where the sound had come from.

"Mark," he said. "Is that you, Alpo-breath?"

Again he heard it, faint and far away. A cat?

"Are you chasing cats again, Purina-lips?" Skip asked. He got up and flung open the door of his room.

The hall was dark. And silent as a grave.

The wail was louder this time. It hadn't come from inside the house.

A sudden shiver ran down Skip's back.

Reluctantly he turned and walked back into his room. He pushed the Save button on the computer.

"Helllp! Help meeeee!" he heard. The sound was coming from outside his window.

He stared at the half-drawn curtains for a long moment. At last he walked over and flattened himself against the wall next to the window. He leaned forward slightly and peered around the edge of the window, twitching aside a corner of the curtain.

For a second all he saw was the square of light from his window falling onto the grass two floors below.

Then a little girl ran into the light, her long hair streaming out behind her, the full skirts of her dress swirling around her calves. He caught a glimpse of petticoat, a flash of an old-fashioned, ankle-high shoe with buttons.

She stopped.

She looked wildly around. She flung out her arms and raised her face. Her eyes were wide with panic. She stared up at the window. She lifted her hands beseechingly toward Skip.

"Help meeeee!" she cried.

Forgetting to be afraid, Skip sprang to the window. He pushed it open and leaned out. "What?" he said. "What is it?"

She didn't seem to see him. "Help me!" she cried again, and sank to her knees. Bringing one trembling hand to her face, she pointed up the road toward the dead end. "It missed the turn. It missed the sign. The bridge is out!"

"What are you talking about? That's a dead end," Skip said.

"Help me," she moaned. "Help—"

"Stay right there," Skip ordered. "I'm coming down."

He closed the window and ran from the room. He took the stairs two at a time, not caring how much noise

76

he made. Had there been an accident? What if someone was hurt?

He flung open the front door and raced out into the night.

She was still kneeling in the square of light. She had both hands over her face now and was crying. "The turn, the turn," she wept. "It missed the turn."

"Calm down," said Skip. "What turn?"

She didn't answer.

"Listen, it'll be all right," Skip said. "I'll get my parents, we'll call for an ambulance . . ." He slowed to a walk as he went toward her, trying to sound calm, trying not to panic.

"The coach," she moaned.

"Who?" Skip asked, startled. "Our soccer coach?"

She rocked back and forth as Skip stopped next to her. "Don't worry," he said. "It'll be all right."

He reached down awkwardly to pat her shoulder.

And she vanished.

CHAPTER
10

Skip froze, his arm in midair. Slowly he looked around.

He could see no sign of the girl, hear no sound.

"Hey," he said. "Is this some kind of a joke?"

Then he looked down at his hand and realized it was freezing, numb with cold as if he had plunged it into ice water.

"This is *funny*," he said, but his voice cracked. He lowered his hand and began to rub it with his other hand. The warmth returned, making his fingers tingle. He turned in a circle, staring into the darkness that surrounded the square of light from his window.

He'd never seen such a still, dark night. Such a still, dark, *haunted* night.

A hand touched his arm. Skip leaped into the air with a night-rending scream.

His little brother stood there.

"Will you stop doing that?" Skip shouted angrily as soon as he could breathe again.

Mark looked puzzled.

The light in their parents' room came on, and another square of light fell onto the grass below at the other end of the house. Mr. Wolfson raised the window and leaned out. "Skip? Is that you?"

"Yeah," said Skip.

"Me too," said Mark.

"What are you boys doing up?" Mr. Wolfson asked. He sounded more sleepy than annoyed.

"I . . ." Skip scoped the area one last time. Nothing but dark, and he had a hunch it would stay that way until morning. "I thought I heard someone. But I was wrong."

"Go back to bed," Mr. Wolfson ordered. He watched as Skip and Mark walked into the house. Then he shut the window with a bang.

"Was it a burglar?" asked Mark hopefully.

"No."

"Was it a ghost?"

"No!"

"Maybe you were sleepwalking."

"Maybe you should go to sleep," Skip answered grouchily. He went into his room, slammed the door in his brother's face, and locked it.

He crossed to the window and stared down into the night.

He knew what he'd seen.

A ghost.

Great, thought Skip. *We didn't move to a haunted house, we moved to a haunted neighborhood.*

"Let me get this straight," Tyson said. He grabbed the basketball from Skip's hand, dropped it onto his foot, flipped it over his shoulder, and caught it as he whirled around.

"Hey," Skip complained. "This is basketball. No feet."

"Sorry." Tyson gave Skip a smug smile, then shot. "Awright! Two points."

Tyson had talked Skip into a game of one-on-one. But it was hard for Skip to concentrate. He felt sleepy. Tired. Confused. And haunted.

He didn't feel like talking about any of these things.

"Check it out," Tyson said, dribbling the ball under one leg.

"High kick," Skip retorted, and grabbed Tyson's ankle. Hopping off balance, Tyson let go of the ball. Skip released Tyson, grabbed the ball, and made for the basket.

He missed the shot.

"Cheaters never win," Tyson said in his best Polly Hannah imitation.

Skip batted the ball away in disgust and walked to the edge of the court.

"Whoa!" Tyson caught the ball and followed Skip. They sat down on a bench. "Why so rude, dude?"

With a heavy sigh, Skip said, "I'm being haunted. Isn't that enough?"

Tyson caught on immediately. "You had another sighting. Another incident? What? When? You and that bus did the ghost dance this morning?"

"No. It was just an ordinary disgusting bus ride," Skip said. "This was last night."

"What happened?"

Skip told Tyson about the girl and how she had vanished at his touch.

"You touched her? You touched a *ghost*? You are brave, Skip. Definitely."

If he had been less rattled, Skip might have enjoyed the compliment. But he shook his head. "I didn't know she was a ghost until she disappeared. I didn't touch her, either. When I reached out, she just vanished. Dematerialized. Vaporized." He held up his hand. "My fingers felt frozen, too."

Tyson nodded and bounced the ball a couple of times. "Happens when you soak your digits in ectoplasm," he said. "You know, ghost flesh."

"I know what ectoplasm is," Skip said.

"Right. You've been pressing the ectoplasm with every ghost in town lately, haven't you?" Tyson sounded slightly envious.

"The point is," Skip went on, "that it's getting worse. Three sightings in two days. A new ghost. What else is going to happen? I can't take much more of this,

82

always looking over my shoulder, always wondering what will happen next . . .''

"Yeah. Like, you open your locker and *bam,* something big and mean jumps out," Tyson agreed. "Or you sit up one morning and put your feet over the side of the bed and *zap,* it grabs you by the ankles. Or—"

Skip stood up. "Do you mind? You are no help," he said.

Tyson stood up too. "Hey, what do you want me to say? Hire a ghost-hunter? I'm not saying a ghost-hunter couldn't get a lot of business around here, but I don't think there are any."

This was true.

Skip walked back to the court. Park and Algie came bombing toward them. "Two-on-two!" shouted Park. "Us against you. Baseball versus soccer."

"You could ask this ghost what it wants," said Tyson behind Skip.

"I tried talking to the girl," said Skip. "She just disappeared. And I'm not going to stand in the road talking to a bus that only I can *see.*" After all, when he'd tried to confront the bus, it had just run over him. He grabbed the ball out of Tyson's hands and fired it across the court to Park.

"Maybe not. But what if you stopped running away from the bus?"

"Tried that, remember?"

"But what if instead of challenging it, or threatening

83

it, you tried to talk to it. Or if you see the girl again, maybe you could . . ." Tyson's voice trailed off.

"Ask her if she's having a bad day? Give the bus driver a few tips on safe driving? I don't think so."

"Play ball!" Algie shouted.

They ran onto the court. As they did, Skip glanced up the hill toward the graveyard.

Where had she come from, the weeping ghost? For that matter, where had the bus come from?

And why?

Shake it off, he told himself. The ghosts wouldn't follow him to school. Dr. Morthouse was scarier than any ghost, right?

Right.

"Skip!" shouted Tyson, darting up the court.

Skip ran after him.

Tyson lofted the ball into the air toward him. Skip leaped up for it. He froze in midleap.

Then he threw his hands out, punching at the ball and trying to back up in midair. "No!" he shouted as he fell. *"No, no, no!"*

The ball had turned into a giant, grinning head, spinning straight at him.

CHAPTER

11

He stumbled. He sat down hard on the cement. The ball shot over his body with a hiss. It bounced once on the court beside his ear. He thought he heard a faint, menacing chuckle.

He turned his head.

A face leered at him. A face with only one eye. And then that mad blue eye winked.

"No!" Skip rolled away, giving the ball a punch in the nose. Tyson tripped over Skip. Park crashed into Tyson.

"What're you doing!" Park punched Skip in the arm.

"Will you guys quit lying around and play ball?" Skip heard Algie complain. He picked up the ball and bounced it dangerously close to Skip's ear for emphasis.

Skip flinched. "Get off me!" he shouted.

"My pleasure," said Tyson, pulling free and standing up.

Tyson, Park, and Algie looked down at Skip.

Skip got up.

"What was that all about?" asked Park. "Is this the way you play soccer? Screaming every time you get the ball?"

Tyson snickered. "Yeah. He screams for help. 'Cause he doesn't know what to do."

Skip didn't answer. His gaze was fastened on the ball, which Algie was bouncing up and down, up and down.

An ordinary orange-brown basketball, regulation size. The only marks on it were the brand name and the scuffs from hours of playing hoops.

Tyson had been joking about a ghost in his locker.

But it was no joke. It could happen.

Anything could happen now.

The ghosts had followed Skip to school.

"Skip?"

Skip turned the page of his math book as if he were really doing homework. He wasn't. He was brooding. And ignoring his mother.

"Skip!"

Footsteps came down the hall.

Was he safe in his room? Was he safe anywhere? The answers weren't in his math book, that was for sure. Why didn't they ever teach anything useful at school, like Introduction to Dealing with Ghosts or Advanced Poltergeist Problem Solving?

"Skip!"

If you had two ghosts and you divided them by one bus, how many ghosts did you have? Who knew? Maybe ghosts multiplied by division, the way those cells they studied in science did. Clone ghosts.

A parade of protoplasm.

"Skip." His mother's voice sounded annoyed. He turned. She was standing in his doorway. She put her hands on her hips. "Didn't you hear me calling you?" Before Skip could answer, she said impatiently, "Never mind. Would you go get Mark and Lupe, please? They're over at Mrs. Strega's, and it's almost time for dinner."

"Can't you just call?"

"I did. There's no answer. They must be out on the farm somewhere."

"Leave a message on her answering machine," said Skip. He glanced at the window. It was getting late. If the ghosts were gathering by day at the playground, who knew what they were planning under cover of darkness?

"She doesn't have an answering machine, Skip." Now his mother sounded really annoyed.

With an exaggerated sigh, Skip stood up. "Okay. I can always stay up extra late to do my homework. Don't worry about me."

"I won't," said his mother.

Skip edged out the back door. Still daylight. But the shadows were gathering. And he didn't like the look of them.

He hesitated. Should he make a run for it and take his chances? Or walk slowly, trying to watch his back?

He decided to walk. He let the back door close—and then took off. He charged down the driveway, across the road, and up the hill to Mrs. Strega's farm. He thundered up the front steps and pounded on her front door.

The sound echoed hollowly through the house. When no one answered he called, "Mark! Mrs. Strega!"

No answer again. He heard the cows and made a face. He turned and pressed his back against the door, measuring the distance to the barn. His brother and Mrs. Strega were probably out there, feeding the cows. Lupe would be rolling in manure and feeling like the coolest dog around. If he knew his little brother, Mark was probably also rolling around in manure and feeling frisky about the whole thing.

Skip leaped off the porch and ran to the barn.

And stopped just outside the door, a chill creeping along his spine.

Something strange loomed by the side of the barn in the evening. Something large and yellow and eerily familiar.

A school bus.

Skip swallowed hard. He blinked. He looked away and looked back again, just to make sure.

His eyes hadn't deceived him. He was face to headlight with a yellow school bus.

"Skip. Hi! I helped feed the chickens!" Mark came bouncing toward him with Lupe.

"Chickens?" Skip repeated mechanically.

"And roosters. They really do crow in the morning. I'm going to listen for them."

"Roosters," Skip said.

Mrs. Strega came out of the barn behind Mark and Lupe. "Hello, Skip."

Skip tore his gaze from the school bus. "Uh, hi, Mrs. Strega. Is—Is that yours?"

"Sure is," she said.

"Does it . . ." Skip swallowed hard. "Does it work?"

Mrs. Strega laughed. "No."

"Are you sure?"

"Take a look for yourself."

Skip hesitated. Every instinct warned him to stay away from the bus.

"It's a cool bus," Mark told him. Mark raced forward and pulled on the bus door. It opened with a shriek and a groan. He climbed up the stairs. He poked his head through the front window.

"What— Be careful!" Skip gasped.

"Look, Skip! No windows!" said Mark.

"No tires to speak of, either," remarked Mrs. Strega. She led the way to the bus. Weeds grew all around it. Many of the windows were missing. The faded yellow paint had rusted away in big, mangy-looking patches. The tires were flat.

"You seem surprised," said Mrs. Strega, watching Skip closely.

"I, uh, just saw a bus like that. At Ken Dahl's . . ."

Mrs. Strega nodded. "The county sold all the old buses years ago, when they bought new ones. My father went to the auction, don't ask me why." She patted the bus. "It stopped working years ago. But I used to play in it and take great imaginary trips."

"This is excellent!" Mark shouted, poking his head out of another window.

"It doesn't work," Skip said, just to be sure.

"Hasn't since I was a girl," Mrs. Strega answered.

"Like for years and years and years?"

"Something like that," she agreed.

"Vrooom, vroom, vroom! Sit down in back!" Mark said. He'd taken the driver's seat and was hunched over the wheel. "Honk, honk! Out of my way!"

Even though Mark was only playing, it was giving Skip the creeps. "Mark, get down from there. It's time to go home," he said.

"Be careful," Mark warned, pretending to steer the bus toward Skip.

"Get out! Now!" Skip shouted, leaping back in spite of himself.

Mrs. Strega and Mark both gave Skip surprised looks. But Mark got out of the bus. "We have to

90

get home for dinner," Skip said, trying to sound calm.

The three of them walked toward the road. Mark said, "Can I come tomorrow? May I?"

"Sure," said Mrs. Strega.

Skip looked at the old farmer. Hadn't she said something about this area's being haunted? "Go on home," he said to Mark. "I'll be right there. I just want to ask Mrs. Strega a question."

Surprisingly, Mark didn't argue. He took off, with Lupe at his heels.

"What did you want to ask me?"

Skip stopped. He suddenly felt foolish. How did he begin? "Excuse me, but I'm being followed by an insane school bus"? "I see ghosts"? "A ghostly school bus followed me home"?

"Uh, well, you've lived here all your life, right?"

"And then some," Mrs. Strega said, with a dry laugh. "Years and years and years."

"Right." He'd long since learned to ignore the adult idea of humor. He also observed that adults were funny about things like age and weight. He decided not to ask Mrs. Strega how old she was—or, for that matter, how much she weighed.

Instead he said, "You said something about ghosts the other day when you came to visit."

"Did I?" She was watching him closely now. It made him uncomfortable.

91

"Yeah. So I was just wondering if you had seen any."

"Ghosts?"

"Uh-huh. Like, you know, a little girl, maybe, running up to your house, for example. Screaming for help. Saying something about a turn and a coach. Just as an example," he added. "I'm not saying I saw that or anything."

Mrs. Strega scratched her chin. "Funny you should mention it. My great-aunt, who was very old when I was a little girl, told the same story."

A chill crept up Skip's spine. "S-She did?"

"Oh, yes. Of course, she didn't tell the story about seeing the ghost. She told the story because she was the little girl."

"Your aunt was a *ghost*?" Skip practically screamed.

"Did I say that? I don't think I did." Mrs. Strega tapped her chin thoughtfully. "No, I didn't. My aunt wasn't a ghost. At the time she told the story, she was a very old woman. And very much alive."

Get a grip, Skip told himself. Clenching his hands in his pockets, he said as calmly as he could, "What was the story?"

"When my aunt was a little girl living here, this road was a main road, which were called post roads back then. An inn stood where your house is now. People traveled by horse-drawn coaches, and sometimes coach drivers used to stop at the inn to pick up passengers."

"Like a bus station," said Skip.

"Yes. Anyway, one day the bridge up the road, just over the hill, washed out. A sign was put up pointing travelers along the Post Road to a detour.

"The coach driver made a special stop that same day at the inn to pick up a passenger. But the passenger was late. The driver refused to wait. He flew into one of his terrible rages, got into his coach, and drove the horses out of the inn yard at a gallop before anyone could tell him about the detour.

"My aunt was outside playing when she saw the coach go by. She knew the coachman by his long, black hair and bristly mustache—and the eye patch over his right eye. He was going at a wicked speed, as he always did. He was the sort of man who wasn't afraid of anything, not even death itself. Some people said he'd made a bargain with Death, giving his right eye as down payment. But of course, no one dared ask."

"Mad John," whispered Skip.

Mrs. Strega looked at him and nodded. "You've heard of him then." She went on with her story.

"The coach thundered by. My aunt realized that Mad John was driving so fast he hadn't seen the sign warning the bridge was out. He drove the horses straight up the hill instead of turning back.

"She jumped up and tried to stop him, called and screamed and waved.

"But Mad John drove on. So she chased the coach, running as fast as her legs would carry her. But it was no use. The coach flew over the hill—and disappeared from sight.

"She heard a horrible howl and what sounded like a cry of 'Oh, no you don't!'

"When she reached the top of the hill, the coach was nowhere in sight.

"She ran back to the inn to get help. But when the people reached the washed-out bridge, they saw no sign of Mad John or his coach in the ravine below, not a coach wheel or even a scrap of wood floating on the river at the bottom.

"Nothing was ever seen of the coach or the passengers or Mad John again."

"The coach," said Skip softly. "She said something about the coach. I thought she was talking about our coach at Graveyard School."

He looked up. It was getting late. He had to go. But he had to ask one last question. "Has anyone ever seen a ghost of, you know, Mad John?"

Mrs. Strega gave a bark of laughter. "Some people used to say he stopped along the road and offered people a ride in his coach." She laughed again, although Skip didn't see what was so funny. "My aunt believed he was looking for that last passenger. But then, who would get on an old-fashioned horse-drawn coach these days? A good thing, too, because if my aunt was right, a ride with Mad John would be the last ride you'd ever take."

CHAPTER

12

"The last ride," Skip said, almost to himself.

"My great-aunt never forgot. She always thought that if Mad John had waited to pick up that last passenger, he might have heard about the bridge from someone at the inn. If he'd done that, he might not have missed the turn."

"The last ride."

"Yep." Mrs. Strega turned to go into her house. "Of course, no one's seen the coach for a long time now. Maybe his ghost just got tired. I guess that could happen."

"I guess," Skip said.

"Night," said Mrs. Strega, and went into the house. The slamming of the door brought Skip back to the present with a start. He realized how late it had gotten.

He stared across the road and down the hill toward his house. It was so near, and yet so far away.

He took off and ran home as fast as he could.

Nothing followed him.

For one more night, at least, he wasn't taking a last ride with Mad John.

"Skip! Rise and shine!" A fist thumped his door.

He lifted the pillow and called, "I don't have to get up yet. School doesn't start for hours!"

"The bus will be here before then. And you can't miss it. I have to take Mark to the dentist, and your mother has to make an early delivery," his father called back.

"Yeah, right," Skip muttered. "I forgot they had to file down his fangs."

Another great thing about living miles from nowhere—he got to get up early just to ride the bus.

Or get run over by one.

That woke him up.

Did he believe in ghosts, or was he letting his imagination run away with him? As he got ready for school, he tried to think things through logically.

He was being haunted by a school bus.

Or else someone with an old school bus was driving around the country trying to run him over. Was it someone who had bought one of the old buses that had gotten sold?

He'd seen a ghost run up to the back door.

Or he'd imagined it.

But how were the two connected? Were they connected? Did he believe in ghosts?

He looked at himself in the mirror. "Yes," he said. "I do."

He yawned until his jaws cracked and his eyes watered. He was tired. He'd had trouble falling asleep. His mind kept going around in circles. How many ghosts were haunting him? Why had he seen Mad John's face on the basketball? Was he about to see a ghostly coach and horses?

Maybe the bus will crash into the coach, he thought. *That might solve some problems.*

He walked down the driveway and stopped, checking things out in both directions. The road was empty.

In a farther field, the cows were wading through the grass, looking contented.

No ghost bus sneaking silently up on him. The road was coach-free. He felt smug, for some reason.

And just at that moment, he saw the Graveyard School bus come over the hill and head for the bus stop.

His sense of smugness vanished. The bus was early!

Forgetting about the ghost bus, Skip began to run as fast as he could toward the bus stop.

The bus slowed down. Skip waved his arms wildly as he ran. "Wait!" he gasped. "Wait!"

It stopped. The doors opened.

He was almost there. He'd make it. He wouldn't be late for school.

The doors closed. The bus groaned forward.

"Nooo," Skip howled. "No, wait for me."

He caught up to the bus as it pulled away in a cloud of dust. He ran alongside it, dust in his eyes and his throat, panic in his heart.

If he was late to school again, Dr. Morthouse would kill him. And that was only if she was in a good mood.

"Wait!" he gasped. He pounded on the door of the bus. "Stop! Let me in."

The bus went faster.

"No," Skip said. "Pleeease . . ."

It stopped so suddenly that he almost ran past it. He stopped too, and bent over to try and catch his breath.

The doors wheezed open. Skip straightened up and grabbed them, holding them so that they couldn't close on him. He hurled himself up the steps and onto the bus.

The bus doors closed. Skip fell into the nearest seat. He leaned back, gasping for air, as the bus picked up speed.

"Whew," said Skip to the kid sitting next to him. "I didn't think I'd make it. This bus driver is seriously twisted."

The kid was looking out the window. "Twisted," the

98

kid echoed hollowly, without even turning his head. The kid was wearing a baseball cap turned backward and a turtleneck sweater. He had a skateboard clamped between bony, blue-jeaned legs.

"Yeah, twisted. Like not wrapped right, you know? Not playing with a full deck. A three-wheeler, you know? I mean, what kind of bus driver would just go off and leave a kid? And I wasn't even late."

Peering past the kid's skinny shoulder, Skip frowned. "Is this the right way?" he asked.

The kid shrugged.

The trees began to blur together. The bus seemed to sway from side to side.

"Whoa. Excuse me, but aren't we going a little fast?"

The kid shrugged again.

Skip frowned. What was wrong with this kid? For that matter, what was wrong with this bus driver? They were definitely going fast. Really fast.

"Not that I wanted to ride this bus anyway," Skip muttered.

That got the kid's attention.

He turned to face Skip. "You didn't want to ride this bus?" he asked. He grinned a horrible grin. "Too bad."

Skip screamed.

CHAPTER
13

The skeleton grinned at him with huge, rotten, yellow teeth.

Skip leaped to his feet. The bus veered. It threw Skip across the aisle. He fell on top of another kid.

A hand dripping foul green slime caught his arm. "Hey," a voice rasped in his ear. "Watch where you're falling."

Skip turned and got a faceful of dead breath from a creature that had once been human. But no more. It looked as if it were melting, its puke-green flesh trickling in disgusting waxen blobs from its face, its hand, even its ears.

Reeling back, Skip felt something clasp his shoulder. He half turned and froze. "Wh-What are you?"

"A ghoul," said the creature. "What are you?"

"Human," said Skip.

The ghoul leaned forward. "Not for long," it breathed.

Skip tore free and turned to run. A quick dive through the emergency door, never mind how much of his skin he had to leave on the road, and—

He stopped. He gasped. He gagged.

He was surrounded by them. Creatures from beyond the grave.

Something without a head sat two seats back. Something holding an eye in each hand was hanging over the back of another seat. The eyes blinked and stared at him.

A swarm of small, vaguely crablike things scuttled wildly between two seats, playing a gruesome game of tag.

Something touched his ankle, curled around it. He looked down to see a tentacle like an octopus's twining up his leg.

"No!" Skip leaped back, shaking his leg frantically. He tore loose and rolled over onto his hands and knees. He kicked out at the curling tentacle. "Take a dive, you swamp booger!" he shouted.

He scrambled forward. The front door. He had to make it to the front door. It was the only way to escape this nightmare.

Nightmare. That was it. He was dreaming. At any moment he would wake up.

But he didn't. The dirty floor of the bus was real against his hands and knees. The skull leaning forward to stare down at him from its seat was not just a night fright.

His worst dream had come true. He'd gotten on the wrong bus.

He had to get off.

The skeleton reached out with a bony finger. Skip leaned sideways and, still on his hands and knees, slithered away from it. He felt something brush along his spine, felt something grasp his sweatshirt.

"Oh no you don't," he gasped, and jerked free.

Somehow, he reached the front of the bus. He got to his knees. He grabbed the railing on the back of the driver's seat to steady himself.

"Help," he said weakly. "Help me."

The bus driver shifted gears. The bus tipped onto two wheels and rocked around a curve.

"Help me," Skip pleaded.

The driver wrenched the wheel. The bus went four-wheels-to-earth with a thud.

Only then did the driver turn his head.

"Sit down," he ordered in a cold, dead voice.

Skip froze. He opened his mouth to scream. He heard his throat make a noise like a broken whistle.

The bus driver had one mad blue eye, a black mustache hanging under his nose like a bad-luck horseshoe—and a patch where the other eye should have been.

"Sit down," said the bus driver again.

"M-Mad John!" Skip cried.

A hand shot out and caught Skip by the neck of his sweatshirt. Mad John lifted Skip until his feet dangled above the floor of the bus. He stared deep into Skip's eyes with his one blue eye. "Pleased to meet you. How'd you guess my name?" The dead coachman grinned. He licked his lips. "You're a fat one, aren't you?"

"No!" said Skip.

Mad John gave Skip a little shake. With his other massive hand, he gave the wheel another twist.

The bus veered along the edge of the road, knocking out a mailbox and flattening a small bush.

"Are you arguing with *me*?"

"Uh, no," Skip managed to choke out.

They reached the top of the hill and sailed upward. The bus hung in the air for several seconds. Through the window behind Mad John's head, Skip could see a valley stretched out below, full of peaceful farms and green pastures filled with cows.

"You'd better *not* be arguing with me," Mad John growled. His breath was the worst breath of all, the breath of someone who gargled with grave juice.

Skip tried not to gag. "But you—you—you're dead," he said.

Mad John gave Skip another shake. The bus landed with a bone-jarring thud.

Skip heard something crunch and shatter. A skull bounced up the aisle and rebounded off his leg.

"Pick it up!" Mad John ordered, without taking his eyes off Skip.

Straining to see out of the corners of his eyes, Skip caught a glimpse of a skeletal hand. It groped along the floor until the finger bones closed around the skull. The skull and the hand disappeared from his sight.

The bus bounced again, and Skip flew upward. Mad John rose too, still holding on to Skip. They floated in midair, eye to eye. The dead man's grip was incredibly strong.

"You're dead," Skip said again.

"So?" Mad John snarled. "You got a problem with that?"

"N-No. No. Uh, no, sir!" said Skip.

The dead coachman gave the steering wheel a kick. The bus ricocheted across the road and back again. "Good," he said.

Skip closed his eyes and tried to think of something good. Like not dying.

When he opened them again, Mad John threw back his head and laughed fiendishly. "You're not scared, are you, little boy?"

Forgetting that he was being held in a death grip in midair, Skip jerked backward. "Who're you calling little?"

Mad John let him go, and Skip crashed to the floor of the bus again. He sensed rather than saw things tumbling into the aisle and beginning to move toward him.

The ghost resumed his seat at the wheel of the bus. "Sit down!" he roared.

The movement behind Skip stopped. Mad John pointed to the seat behind the driver. "Sit down," he said again.

"If you don't mind," Skip said, "I think I'd like to get off the bus now. It's been an *interesting* ride and all, but—"

"*Sit!*"

Skip sat.

"It *is* an interesting ride," Mad John said calmly.

Skip looked out the window. Farms. Pastures. Cows. "Been there, done that," he muttered, trying to regain some grip on reality.

Mad John slammed on the brakes. The bus reeled around a corner. Skip gasped.

He wouldn't have thought it was possible to be more terrified, but he was.

The bus had turned onto Post Road.

"I hate passengers who aren't on time," the coachman roared. He accelerated up the hill.

"Wait!" cried Skip. "Slow down!"

"Hate people who tell me what to do!" The bus picked up speed.

"No! Stop!"

"Hate people who don't listen."

The bus flew by Skip's house.

They were headed straight up the hill. And Skip knew without ever having seen it that on the other side, the road went straight down to a bridge that wasn't there.

CHAPTER
14

"It doesn't get any deader than this!" the coachman shouted.

"Stop!" Skip said. "No! The road is *closed.* The bridge is *out!*"

Mrs. Strega's farm flashed by. For a moment Skip thought he saw Mrs. Strega standing there, staring. Then she was gone.

"Stop! We'll be killed!"

Laughter erupted from the back of the bus. To Skip's horror, the driver took both hands off the wheel and turned. He gave Skip a hearty whack on the shoulder. "Good one!" he said.

"No, listen! You have to listen! There's a sign, see? It says 'Road Closed. Dead End.' "

" 'Dead End'!" someone—or something—behind Skip sang out. Gibbering giggles answered.

"Stop, stop, *stop!*"

"I am *tired* of going the same way over and over," a voice rasped in Skip's ear.

"We've been doing it forever," another voice rasped in agreement. "Boring!"

But as softly as the voices had spoken, Mad John had heard. He spun all the way around in his seat. Then he rose out of the seat straight into the air. His face turned bloodred. His blue eye popped out of its socket on a bloody stalk.

"What did you say?" he roared in rage. *"I hate criticism!"*

"It's true," another voice said.

"Arrrrrgh!" screamed the insane driver.

Skip saw his chance. He bent and lunged forward. Something raked his back. He heard Mad John roar again.

Skip got his hands on the wheel. It was as cold as ice. Yet burning steam poured off it.

"Owww!" screamed Skip, but he held on. He turned the wheel of the bus. It seemed to fight back.

"Unhand my vehicle!" Mad John screamed in Skip's ear.

They reached the top of the hill.

Brakes, thought Skip. *I have to find the brakes.*

He slid into the seat. Icy coldness closed around his body like a claw.

A hand clamped onto his wrist, a big, hairy, ugly, powerful hand.

He slid forward, searching for the brake with both feet.

The hand gave his wrist a bone-cracking twist. "Let go of that wheel," a deadly voice murmured in his ear.

"Oh, no!" someone cried shrilly. "Oh, no, oh, no! *The bridge is out!*"

At that moment, Skip's foot found the brake. He mashed it down with all his might, throwing his weight sideways as he wrenched the wheel of the bus.

The back of the bus swung out. They went down the last part of the road sideways. Screams and wails filled the air.

Skip watched the edge of the ravine coming closer. Closer. Closer.

He gave the wheel one last jerk and closed his eyes.

He was going to die.

Roaring filled his ears. Lightning flashed in the darkness behind his eyelids.

And then he knew no more.

His head hurt. He smelled like a dead swamp. He raised his head and squinted.

He was late for school.

"Uhnnnhh," he groaned, and let his head fall back.

He was sprawled against the steps of Graveyard School. The steps were empty, except for him and his backpack, which was spilled open nearby.

Slowly he dragged himself to his feet. Weaving and

staggering, he gathered his things together and crammed them back into the pack.

When he reached the door, he took a long breath, trying to think. But it was hard to think clearly. The last thing he remembered was holding the steering wheel of the runaway bus.

How had he gotten to school? Had he been running up the stairs and slipped and fallen? Hit his head and imagined the whole thing?

He sniffed. The smell was real. No way he could imagine that combination of rotten dead thing and swamp brew. It was the smell of the inside of the bus.

Still dazed and confused, he opened the door and walked into the school. After everything that had happened, the halls suddenly looked good to him. He couldn't believe it. He was actually glad to see the green walls and the battered lockers, to catch the scent of the dirty water that Basement Bart used to wash the floors.

He was alive, he suddenly realized. Not dead. He'd escaped the bad-news bus. Gone eye to eye with Mad John and lived to tell about it.

His ride on the bus hadn't been his last ride after all.

Oh, yes. It was good to be alive. At that moment, he loved Graveyard School and everything in it.

And a hand fell on his shoulder.

"Well, well, well, Skip, what have we here?" purred a soft, nasty, familiar voice. "Late *again*?"

Skip looked up. He met Dr. Morthouse's mean, cold eyes. She smiled her silver-fanged smile.

He gave her a giddy smile in return. "Dr. Morthouse! You look great! It's so good to see you!" He flung his arms around the principal of Graveyard School in a bear hug.

Dr. Morthouse made a sound that might have been a shriek. She leaped back so quickly that Skip lost his grasp and reeled against the lockers on one wall.

Keeping her eyes on Skip's face, Dr. Morthouse backed against the lockers on the other wall. Her mouth opened and closed soundlessly. She lifted one shaking hand and wiped a bead of sweat from her forehead.

She took a deep breath and seemed to recover her senses. *"Go. To. Class. Now!"* she thundered.

Skip had recovered his senses too. What had he been thinking?

He took off before Dr. Morthouse could change her mind.

Mrs. Strega looked up as Skip walked into the barn. She wiped her hands on her overalls and waited.

"You saw the bus this morning, didn't you?" asked Skip.

The farmer nodded. "Yep. Saw it go up the hill. Saw it come back down."

"Did you see who was driving?"

She nodded again. "Mad John," she said matter-of-factly. Then she added, "So that's what happened to that other school bus."

"Other bus?" Skip's voice went up. "What other bus? What are you talking about?"

"We bought two, don't ask me why."

"You had two buses and you didn't tell me?" Skip was practically shouting. He'd had a bad day. A very bad day.

Mrs. Strega said calmly, "Didn't seem important. Been gone for years. Never could figure out who'd done it. Or why. Now I guess I know."

"You mind sharing a few answers with me?" asked Skip, not even trying to keep the irritation out of his voice.

But Mrs. Strega didn't seem to notice or care. She picked up a feed bucket and went out into the barnyard. She began to scatter feed for the chickens. "Mad John took it, of course. Couldn't get anybody to get in that coach of his. No one rode in coaches anymore. Course, it wasn't easy to get an adult in the school bus, either."

"So he waited for a kid?" Skip asked.

She didn't answer. She said, "I've seen that coach go up the hill myself, a number of times. Never saw anything come back down. Until today."

Skip said slowly, "He was looking for that last passenger, wasn't he? The one who could have warned him that the road was out."

"Maybe so."

Looking up the hill, Skip said, "I kept the bus from going over the cliff. So I guess he gave me a ride to Graveyard School."

"Or maybe he just dropped you off," said Mrs. Strega quietly. "On his way to rest."

Skip thought of the graveyard behind the school. His eyes widened. "You think . . ." He let his voice trail off.

Then he said, "Thanks." He turned and walked slowly home. He didn't bother to look over his shoulder. He didn't think he'd see the ghost bus ever again.

Mad John's driving days were over. Forever.

EPILOGUE

The doors of the bus wheezed shut. A last passenger squeezed on.

"Hurry up! Hurry up!" the driver called. "Hate late passengers."

It was an old bus but well cared for. Newly painted on the sides were the words TOURS THROUGH TIME AND SPACE. Below that, in smaller letters, it said, STOP ME IF YOU CAN.

The driver threw the bus into gear. The passenger lost his balance and sprawled in the aisle with a clatter of bones.

Mad John floored it. The bus veered around the end of the line of tombstones and shot around Dead Man's Curve. It left the ground completely.

"The road!" a funereal voice groaned. "You've left the road."

"Road? Who needs roads!" Mad John drove the bus through the side of the school and out the other side. He wrenched the wheel, and the bus flew cross-country. "Free!" he shouted. "I'm freeee!"

He turned on the headlights, the window wipers, and the turn signals all at once. He blasted his horn. "Freeeee!"

He made the old run one last time, followed the route he'd driven involuntarily for so long. But he slammed his brakes on at the top of the old Post Road. He turned the bus around.

"Ha!" he shouted. He floored it.

The hill gave him a running start. The front wheels left the road, and then the back ones. Mad John's Tour Through Time and Space took off straight into the sky.

In the farmhouse nearby, Skip mumbled something in his sleep and pulled his pillow over his head.

Mrs. Strega looked out her window and smiled.

And a little girl standing in front of her house opened her eyes wide and raised her arms to wave before she vanished forever.

Ghoulish Word Search!

Find the following words in the puzzle below. Hint: Words can go up, down, diagonally, forward, and backward!

Goblin	Ghoul
Witch	Zombie
Ghost	Monster
Skeleton	Vampire
Werewolf	Warlock

```
R  O  W  E  R  E  W  O  L  F
K  N  V  A  M  P  I  R  E  M
N  C  G  I  E  R  T  O  I  O
G  H  O  S  T  I  C  G  B  N
D  R  B  L  U  O  H  G  M  S
U  E  L  Z  R  H  E  N  O  T
A  N  I  S  Q  A  V  U  Z  E
I  O  N  R  E  E  W  S  C  R
F  S  K  E  L  E  T  O  N  J
```

Tom B. Stone has written more than forty books for children. The author enjoys playing soccer, sailing, reading, hiking, biking, blading, and staying up late. The author does not enjoy anchovies, broccoli, squid, politicians, or scary movies. Tom lives in Sag Harbor, New York, with two dogs and three cats.